ASH ON THE RANGE

RED HART RANCH

SOFIA AVES

Welcome to Red hart Ranch

ASH
ON THE
RANGE
Red Hart Ranch

SOFIA AVES

First Edition

EBOOK ISBN 978-1-923471-90-0

PRINT ISBN 978-1-923471-07-8

CHAPTER ONE

WILL

The drive into Red Hart Ranch was just as I remembered it. Rolling hills were covered in golden grasses still flowering in late fall before winter finally set in. Everything was ablaze in a glory of color until we rounded the bend that brought the familiar sight into view, and although it wasn't a carbon copy, this would aways be the same image I stored in my mind of the first time I saw the ranch of the jaw dropping variety.

The picturesque mountain that watched over the big house, like it studied everything that sat beneath its immense, white capped overhang. The giant red and white RHR sign covered in stylized Imperial antlers surrounded by heavy lettering I'd never forget from my first drive into Red Hart land. That day I'd sat in the back of one of the farm trucks along with a dozen other seasonal ranch hands hired on by one of the ranch's then heirs and now owners for twelve weeks' worth of work and pay. Solid meals I could count on. Back then, that mattered a lot.

This time, returning to the ranch for my fourth season, it looked a whole helluva a lot different.

This time, I had a stunning girl by my side and a junker of a truck beneath me. But for the first time ever, both were mine.

Cassie's hand flexed around my callused fingers as I pulled up at the gate, craning up at the RHR sign. "Should I be nervous?"

I grinned. "Being here? Nah. The first time I ever pulled through these gates I was on the back of a pick-up packed in like sardines with a dozen other farm hands. I had no idea what I was doin' and less of an idea of what hard work looked like. But it was the best job I'd been given and by the end of the season, I drove back out a different person. Been coming back every season ever since." I squeezed her hand reassuringly. "You wanna grab the gate for me?"

She stayed stock still in the passenger seat, clenching my fingers in a death grip. "So, you're saying...I'm about to meet your unofficial family?"

I snorted. "Honey, this is my family. My real one kicked me out at fifteen. Been on the road ever since. That was the same kid you met out the back of the rodeo circuit last week where your brother beat the crap out of me, just a handful of years on, yeah?"

"That makes it so much better," she whispered, and slipped out of the passenger seat before I could utter another word.

Damnit. That hadn't been the best thing to say, maybe.

Cassie unhooked the chain draped around the gate that, as far as I knew, was never locked. Or, at least, it never had been the entire time I'd been coming out to Red Hart. A big part of me hoped that never changed. I drove onto RHR land for the first time under my own steam. Tension slipped from my shoulders as I leaned out the window, brushing my fingers across Cassie's shoulders as she walked around my side of the truck.

"Like it?" I asked quietly. "I know it's not a rodeo at midnight, but..." That was where I'd met her, a dusty rodeo ground a few starts and a week away. We'd been driving ever since, when I promised her I'd take her somewhere else. Somewhere better. Now we were here, I hoped my promises would be able to live up to reality.

Like me. Will Kirk. The kid who couldn't stay on a bull to save himself. Couldn't stay with a girl, either. Didn't have a home and drifted from place to place, season to season. Sensing a theme there?

I found her hand and squeezed, hoping I didn't hold on half as hard as I strangled the steering wheel.

"It's beautiful, Will." Cassie gifted me one of those smiles that left me without air in my lungs as I stared into eyes the color of the clear Montana sky above us. Pale blonde hair drifted about her face, and my fingers itched to tuck it behind her ears. Her gaze shifted focus over the truck, her brow dipping. "Is it meant to be like that?"

I let her hand go to duck my head, peering through the passenger window at the small stream of smoke wafting over the ridge line at the mountain's foothills that rose along the border of the next property behind Red Hart to the north.

"Shit. Could be back burning. Might be the day for it. But..." *Also, maybe not.* A light breeze feathered across the rise to sway the red and gold grass heads. I doubted Jude would risk a burn today. He was as conservative as it came, and I'd worked with Red Hart's foreman for enough seasons to have a read on him, even half a year apart since I'd seen him last. I doubted he'd recommend it to anyone else, either. My jaw set. "Hop in, Cassie."

She trotted around the front of the truck, and the tension that dropped off my shoulders left me as took off too fast down the long drive, heading toward the main house. The view I'd always appreciated blurred past. Cassie's hand slipped into mine as we headed toward the big house.

I pulled into the yard at a much slower speed, and no intention of dusting the house up. The boys wouldn't appreciate that, and neither would Eve. A few battered trucks, including Trav's old one, were packed by the house that looked just the way I remembered it. A wrap around veranda framed a high peaked roof. Generations of Beaumont history sat right there in front of me watched over by the pensive mountain that never shifted its unerring gaze.

Cassie clung to my hand. "Wow," she whispered. "I know you said... but I didn't think it would be this big."

"It's pretty huge," I muttered. "The first time I turned up here, I didn't think I'd ever be worthy to step foot in the yard, let alone the big house. But we eat there every night, all of us. Eve opens the house up, cooks for everyone. We do things differently here."

She shifted in her seat, tearing her eyes away from the house and the mountain, and I knew the effort that cost because on my first time around, my eyes were goggling out of my head. "This really is your family, isn't it?" She shivered, pulling her hand free and wrapped her arms around herself in a one person hug.

All thought of the fire departed my mind. I reached for her, tugging her close. Neither of us had bothered with seatbelts once we were on the drive and off the black top, making it that much easier to haul her across the bench seat and into my arms.

"You don't need to be scared here, Cass," I murmured, doing what I wanted before and pushing my fingers through her dirty blonde hair to tuck it behind her ear. My fingers continued their trail across her curved cheek, over her jaw, tipping her face up to mine until my mouth covered hers. She sighed, sinking into me.

It had been too long since I kissed her. Hours, maybe. We'd kept things above board since we left the rodeo. It had been rushed there, a bit of hell since her brother took a dislike to me and tried to beat me into the ground with the only thing that worked on him—his fists, since his brain didn't do the job so well. And since we'd only kissed before, that's how we kept it all week, light touches, falling asleep together.

It didn't help that I was still recovering from a dislocated shoulder from the same assholic incident and maybe a bull that threw me the same night. But hell, all that also threw me into the path of the girl in my arms, so who was I to complain?

Soft lips yielded beneath mine. I traced my tongue along hers, then, when she sighed softly for me, delved deeper, squeezing her waist as she leaned into me. Christ, why had we waited again? Something about chivalry came to mind, but every time I kissed her, those thoughts disappeared in lieu of something else. Her hands wound around the back of my neck, tugging me closer until she surrounded me in a swirl of strawberry lip gloss and caramel coffee we picked up in White Cap on our way in.

A bang on the driver's door told me our time was officially up.

I drew back from Cass, stealing a single moment where her eyes were still shut, her lips swollen from our kisses. I kept an arm around her and managed to push the door open with my other hand. Jude, RHR's introvert of a foreman and the most capable teacher I knew, glared at me.

"Hey." I cleared my throat. "Did you know there's a fire up over the northern ridge?"

A muscle in Jude's jaw flickered. I took that as a negative. He jerked his head at Gage, one of Red Hart's older live-in cowboys. He took off on a farm bike, leaving a trail of dust behind him that coated my truck and everything in the yard, including the house, which I'd hoped to avoid, in dust. I winced. "You need a dose of rain, huh?"

"It's good to see you, Will. Now get out of that truck and stop giving the boys a show to prove she's yours." Jude folded his arms over his chest, his glare never wavering.

I grinned, kissed Cass once more fast, and let her go, grabbing my hat and slapped it on my head before I climbed out of my truck.

Jude clapped my shoulder in the sort of friend welcome that might have dislocated the other side if it hadn't been the bruised one.

I grimaced, and rolled the still tender joint. "Do you treat everyone you like that way?"

"A season's work doesn't get done with soft bodies, kid." Jude watched me with a hard eye. "You need the doc to check you out?"

"Nope."

"Because—"

"I'm no good to you injured," I supplied, reaching out to grab my bag from the back of the pickup, twice as glad my back was turned to him when my shoulder did more than twinged when I tried to take the weight of the canvas. "Fuck," I muttered under my breath.

Cass watched me, her gaze narrowed, but thankfully she didn't say anything. Her bright blue eyes told me I'd hear about it later, though if not from Jude then from her.

The foreman was still talking, and the white hot shot of pain that blocked out his words for a moment receded long enough to let me focus on the rest of what he was saying.

"Think you can stay on a bull for long enough not to disgrace the colors, Will, or are you going to stare at a pretty girl for the next few minutes and ignore me?"

I grinned again, swinging around, glad he gave me the out I needed. "What am I doing with a bull that I won't do with a pretty girl?"

A raucous shout went up with the ranch hands already gathered in the yard who I ignored when we pulled up. I'd said the right thing to save my ass from trouble, thankfully. I'd always had an easy going nature here and a reputation for being a bit of a joker, as long as the work got done at the end of the day. Right now, that saved my ass, even if it colored Cass's cheeks before I turned about.

"We're hosting a rodeo here on Red Hart grounds. Figured you'd want in, if you turned up on time. Gonna ride for us, Will Kirk?" A very different voice reached my ears.

I turned away from Jude's weathered facade to face Eve. Chestnut hair curled around her shoulders to just below her waist, longer than I remembered. A pristine white shirt, branded with the RHR antlers was tucked into tight blue jeans and boots I knew Archer had bought for her. I glanced around for him, but she shook her head, her bright smile dimming a little.

"Good to see you, ma'am," I said softly, my heart clenching at the sight of her loneliness.

Cassie was right—Red Hart had become my home at some point in the last few seasons. I swallowed hard on a lump that threatened my next breath as Eve crossed the yard and wrapped her arms around my neck.

"Quick hug, because that pretty girl you've brought with you is burning me to ash right now," she whispered into my ear, and stepped back. "I swear you're getting taller every time you come back here, Will," she announced in a louder voice.

I rubbed the back of my neck that flared with a bout of sudden sunburn. "Yeah, might be," I said, knowing I'd been the same five feet, eleven inches since I'd been sixteen, the year after I left home. I stopped growing and nothing seemed to make that change. I'd come to terms with that in the last seven years or so. Even though I wasn't as tall as Eve's twin, Travis, who strode out of the big house, dwarfing all of us, to clap my shoulder. The not so sore one. I grinned and gave him a nod. "Sir, this is Cassie." I cleared my throat. "I hoped she might be able to stay while I worked for a while?"

I posed the request with as much respect as I could, asking Travis, not Eve, knowing if I asked his sister I'd get a straight out *yes*. But it was Travis I'd be working for over the next however many weeks before I took Cass back to college like we agreed when we left the rodeo grounds a week ago.

Travis held my gaze for a long moment, his lips twitching. "Noticed you turned up with your own truck for once, Mister Kirk."

"Yes, sir."

He turned back, nodding to Cass, then back to me. "It's almost as rusty as mine. You're both welcome as long as you need. She stays in the house. You're in the bunkhouse with everyone else as always, understood?" Two eyebrows hiked to remind me I wasn't to go upstairs with Cass at any point.

House rules were house rules, and upstairs was for family only. Cass got a decent bed though, and that was more than I could ask for.

I breathed out and grinned my relief. "Appreciate it always, sir."

"Good man. Got a few hours left in the day. Are you ready to work?"

"Always." I tossed my bag back on the truck's

flatbed beside Cass's meager things we'd taken from her brother's van before we left the last rodeo.

And now we had our own coming to Red Hart. My shoulder twinged on cue and I rotated the sore joint. A week on the road hadn't done me any favors, but traveling with Cass had been easy. Without her I would have hauled ass across the country, slept on the back of the truck instead of in highway motels, and done the trip in two days. With her...we took our time, and the last week was less a blur than a break in the middle of no man's land for me. Time I shouldn't have stolen with her, but I did anyway.

"He's already started. Says he spotted smoke up on the north ridge. Near the road, right?" Jude stepped in neatly for me.

I nodded, and Travis's naturally hard face cleared. He'd gotten harder after his father was murdered a few seasons ago, and then the twins lost their mother shortly afterward. Tragedy hit Red Hart year after year, but the ranch kept on going. People like Travis and Eve and Jude and even newcomers like Gage who inserted themselves into the landscape like they were part of the dirt kept it going.

Maybe, if I was lucky, one day I'd put down roots somewhere and find myself a -place to call home. If I was twice as lucky, maybe that somewhere would be with someone like Cass. Or just with Cass, period.

One week together and I was already head over heels for the girl who I couldn't keep my hands off. Or my eyes. My gaze kept drifting off toward her, taking my attention with it.

Jude cuffed the back of my head none too gently. "Throw your stuff in the bunkhouse while Eve shows Cassie where she's sleeping. Give yourself ten minutes to get settled, then get your ass back out here, ready to work." The foreman fixed a hard look at me, though the corner of his mouth twitched.

"Yes sir," I said sheepishly, leaning across the tray of the truck to pass Cass her small bag, and tidied up as I grabbed my own.

She looked about nervously as Eve started talking and I got the impression that my girl didn't take in any more information than I had just missed from Just or Trav's pep talks.

"You'll be fine." I stepped up behind Cassie and slipped my arm about her waist, giving her a gentle squeeze. I had less than ten seconds before Jude ripped me a new one for loitering, so I'd make the most of it. "I've never been upstairs. Tell me what it's like." I pressed a kiss to the sensitive spot right below her ear, then let her go, already striding off in the familiar direction of the bunkhouse.

If I hadn't let her go then and there, I wouldn't have let her go at all, and the yard would really have had something to rib me about.

My feet chewed the path I knew well between the big house and where I'd be sleeping for the season. Yet again my heart lamented the time I should have spent in her arms over the last nights, time I wouldn't get now we were on ranch land.

I kicked open the bunkhouse door and was assailed by a strong waft of stale cowboy that rocked me back half a step. Communal living wasn't where it was at.

Yeah, shoulda spent more time in her arms, and skin to skin.

Maybe we'd get some time together over the next weeks while we were here. Red Hart had plenty of romantic places. I huffed a laugh as I threw my bag on the soggiest bunk in the cabin.

Yeah. And maybe Jude will give me a day off with full pay and let me take her on a date for the hell of it.

Because neither of those things were ever gonna happen.

I should have spent more time with her when I had the chance.

I left the bunkhouse at a jog. My ten minutes were nearly up, and I doubted Judge had gotten any softer this season. Maybe if I was real lucky, he'd let me shovel a pile of deer shit, and Cassie could see just how romantic ranch life could be. I clapped my hat on my head and double stepped it back to the barn.

CHAPTER TWO

CASSIE

I hoped my brother turned up at Red Hart for their rodeo. I hoped he walked into the big house and left his jaw on the floor.

Because that's where mine had been when I stepped through those double glass doors—shoes off, of course—after Eve, leaving my jacket on a hook alongside everyone else's. I grew up rich, or thought I did, but Red Hart blew everything right away in my apparently limited experience.

And I wanted to see the day my brother got bitch slapped by a pair of antlers like he deserved for bullying Will, even though the scrappy rodeo cowboy would never admit to it. It hurt seeing Will wince every time he moved or someone touched him, including me, knowing I was responsible for his pain, at least in part.

I focused on that as I toured the enormous bottom floor of the big house, following Eve around as she pointed out the double length table that I could imagine all too easily fitting all the men outside for a single sitting meal laden with table at its heavy wood surface. That matched the kitchen that featured its giant bench top, scarred and worn in its open plan setting across the main area that still left abundant space for chatter and socializing.

Hanging above it all in a cathedral pitched ceiling was a cluster of deer antlers that formed a chandelier above the centre of everything, too big to simply be a feature over one small room, but enough to spread over the entire open space. The effect was awe inspiring. I stood gawking in the appropriate manner, wishing Will was here to tell me that his jaw hit the floor on his first time too, or that he drooled at least a bucket's worth so that I didn't feel so alone.

But in the absence of an overwhelming crowd the room simply.... echoed.

"It can be a bit much," Eve acknowledged my unspoken thoughts. "But when the room is full at night for a meal, well..." she shrugged. "It gets kind of frantic. You'll see."

"And you feed everyone? Will mentioned," I added when she raised an eyebrow.

Eve shrugged, glossy chestnut hair rippling with a silky sheen I could never hope to achieve. My own hair felt limp and lackluster next to this rural goddess.

"My mother did it, back when she..." Eve coughed into her hand and faced me in full. "This ranch has been run by my family going back generations. Right now, Travis and I are the only things holding it up, along with all those people you saw in the yard outside. Red Hart has always been a place where people work hard and are fed well for their efforts. Just because our family line appears to stop here doesn't mean our hospitality will." This last part came out at a rushed pace, her words clicking at the ends.

I blinked. "That's one hell of a mission statement."

Eve huffed a laugh. "It's what I considered putting on the website last night."

I shook my head. "Don't. Please. We can work-shop that. I'm pretty sure of it."

Her laugh this time was a full one. "Are you studying?" She made her way around the edge of the long kitchen bench and flicked on the coffee machine. The rich aroma of fresh heavenly beans filled the space, mingling with the scent of heavy oiled wood.

I leaned over the end of the bench, stretching my legs. After sitting in the car for so long, it felt good to move about. My bag settled at my feet. "Nursing, at Montana U. I'm on break. Semi personal enforced. I...deferred some of my studying to help my brother out. That was where Will found me, at the rodeo circuit and...Now I'm here." I echoed her shrug from earlier.

"He promised to take you back after a stint here?" Even guessed, rummaging about in a cupboard she could barely reach for mugs. The woman was tinier than I was, though I suspected she must have been a good few years older than me.

"Let me help," I offered, bemused when she shook her head, warding me away.

"Nope. My kitchen, my rules," she said firmly, pouring the coffee. "Cream?"

"Black, please."

"Perfect. Did you stop at White Cap?" she asked as I resumed stretching.

"'Last coffee stop up the range'," I quoted Will. "Wasn't bad, either. Some place called Barnies—"

"Beanie's," Eve corrected me.

I grinned. "Beanies. At least they had decent coffee. For a rich kid, my brother can be a tight ass. And my monthly allowance dropped while I wasn't studying so...working for him was my only option." I grimaced.

Eve looked at me shrewdly. "So you need a job while you're here, then?"

"Uh—" I hadn't actually planned that far ahead, stuck on the cowboy who dreamed big and fell hard. In hindsight, that seemed fairly remiss.

"It's okay, Cassie, don't panic. There's always work to be done. You said you're studying nursing, right?"

I nodded, then shook my head. "But I don't think I'm that good with animals," I said in a hurry. "The last cat I held tried to murder me, and I might have accidentally drowned my niece's goldfish."

"In air?"

"In water," I said remorsefully.

"That's quite a talent," Eve observed. "So, you're not keen on animals, just people."

"Mostly helping people achieve healthcare, especially in low socioeconomic areas. It should be available to everyone," I started, turning the mug she passed me in my hands, warming my palms. "I feel the same way about education too, especially at a college level, but you probably don't want to get me started on that subject, unless you've got a lot of alcohol under your belt and are prepared to pass out at least halfway through my diatribe."

Eve watched me thoughtfully. "Not good with animals, passionate about helping others... How are you with websites?" she asked hopefully.

I snorted into my coffee. "Have you given up on yours?"

"Just about." She swirled her mug in her hands. "You picked up my language the moment that you walked in. If you want the job of handling updates on marketing while you're here, I could use the assistance. There might be some other jobs about the place too. Did Will mention how we work here?" That arched eyebrow rose again.

I bet she didn't even have to pluck it.

"He said only the family went upstairs," I recalled, blushing at how he'd kissed me in the car.

"Mmhm." Eve seemed lost in a memory of her own. "There's a spare room up there, but he's right, the ranch hands do have to stay downstairs. The land is pretty spread out. There's two hundred and fifty thousand acres between us and the next property, and there's some stunning places to visit. Make sure Will shows you the creek, and the outcrop. Maybe he could take you on a picnic sometime..." Eve drifted off as she finished her mug and headed around a corner, calling out names. "How many men were in the yard just now?"

I counted imaginary heads, and when I lost count, I stuck my own back out the front door of the big house, but the yard was empty. "Where did everyone go?"

"Oh, they'll be off working," Eve said cheerfully, her arms full of an oversized bowl and what looked like every root vegetable known to human kind.

"Ah, do you want help?"

I stared at the pile of food prep, unsure where to start or what she had planned as she disappeared

back around the corner and returned with a side of—
Actually I had no idea what sort of meat that was,
but whatever it came off, the animal left life huge.

"Nope, I'm good, but thanks." Eve started cheerfully chopping and prepping all by herself in the
empty, enormous house.

It hit me then—this was her life. Everyone else
left to work for the day, doing whatever it was that
they did around the ranch, and she was left here in
the house, cooking and prepping and waiting for
them all to come back. And the marketing and
accounts and branding for the farm and whatever
other things that she did, by the sounds of it.
Without any help at all, from the short time I'd been
about for.

"Um, okay." I edged toward the stairs, bag in my
hand, suddenly as unsure as I had been the moment
that I'd climbed out of Will's rusty truck that had
more character and that he; loved more than
anything glossy and shimmy that my brother had
ever been given in his life. "I'll just—"

"Up the stairs, go along the corridor, third door
on the right. The second door is the guest bathroom.
Have a shower. Soak. I'm sure it's been a long day.
Or week. You can't miss any of it," Eve called me as
the knife came down with the sort of rhythm that

spoke of a woman who was used to hard work and reveled in it.

Eve and Travis obviously had a lot too, but from what I saw they earned every cent, working hard and that *mattered*. She might be alone in the house but she obviously loved what she did. It was on the tip of my tongue to ask if everything was grown here—apart from the meat, obviously they ran deer not whatever was being placed in the world's biggest bake tray as I climbed the stairs, but the moment passed and I moved along with it. I could ask later, maybe.

I made it up the stairs without disgracing myself, and passed a pair of doors closed on the left hand side, and a large bedroom with the door open on the right. That looked like it hadn't been used for a while, the floral cover pulled up neatly. I kept walking, past the bathroom, its door slightly ajar, and found the next room, the last on the right.

That one was shut. I pushed it open to find a double bed set out in the middle of the room, its cream cover decorated with a lace pattern woven through the middle laid out over a green oval rug. Matching curtains were pulled aside to let the afternoon light filter into the room. I placed my bag beside the bed, running my fingers over the sturdy wooden posts that matched the bedside tables, and leaned across to peer out the window.

This room looked over the back of the big house, giving me a view of the forest that led into the foothills of the foreboding mountain that watched over Red Hart Ranch like a sleepless sentinel. Unlike the front of the house that viewed the gold and green pastures where the deer grazed, still filled with wildflowers, my view was all evergreen conifers. I imagined it lit with snow in winter, all white caps and icicles. A chill breeze wrapped around me as the sun hid behind a cloud on cue.

Recalling Eve's offer of a shower that suddenly seemed attractive after a week of doubtful motel basin washes that occasionally had hot water, I scrounged through my bag for fresh-ish clothes. Pulling out my only other pair of jeans that I'd managed to dry in the back of Will's truck the day before, I found a lace, long sleeved top plus a knitted white hoodie that I could shrug over the whole lot later on once the sun set.

My meager supplies looked a whole lot less than necessary once I walked into Eve's 'spare' bathroom that held everything anyone ever needed. It was like walking into a shopping mall, with everything laid out on display. I'd grabbed a few things with my remaining cash in White Cap, but the prices had been high, being a small town, and I'd put more than one thing back. Will offered to pay, but I refused his help outright. The shower beckoned. And I stepped in, forgetting my worries for a few minutes as heat drenched me all over. I washed my hair, shaved everything and scoured my body with soap. The result was a squeaky clean me I barely recognized a few minutes later, grateful for hot water that didn't run out though I was conscious of not using it endlessly.

By the time I dressed, unpacked and headed downstairs, the basket of food Eve had been prepping was in the oven and the whole house smelled nothing short of delicious. Eve sat at the gigantic table, a laptop open in front of her.

"Coffee?" I called, finding the mug I used before and pointing to the coffee machine.

Her head raised, and she looked up at me, startled. "Yes, please." Eve smiled, though it strained at the edges. "I was just... We should get you logged into the website. Feel better after the shower?" She stretched her arms over her head, though her face tightened and she dropped her hand to her stomach.

I didn't say anything, turning away to focus on the coffee machine and its many functions. *Not my business. Not my family.* But it was Will's, in a way, and he did offer to share it with me. I closed my eyes once I managed to get the coffee brewing, though it took me a few tries. "Okay, I am no barista," I apologized, placing a fresh mug in front of Eve. "Feel free to hurl it at me any time."

"Mmhm." She made that noise she'd made before, absently clicking her laptop, then pulled a second one from under the tablet. "I made you a cheat sheet." A laminated sheet with passwords and logins was placed on top of the laptop. "This should be everything you need while you're here. That way if you get stuck between us we aren't resetting things every day, okay?"

I stared. "Um, okay?" Tracing over the sheet, I ran through the list. *Website, email, banking?* "Uh, Eve? There's a lot of trust passing across here. I'm not sure I want to handle all of this," I tried, pushing the sheet back to her.

She offered me a tired smile. "Will trusts you, Cassie. Maybe you should ask him a bit about Red Hart sometime. Some of the things we've experienced together here. It might.. Put everything into perspective."

"Oh." The knot that had crept into my heart when Eve hugged Will in the house yard wrapped its tendrils tight once against and pulled tight. "Um, I will. So, where do we start?" I forced a light, cheery note into my voice that insisted on straining as much as Eve's as I sat beside her and opened the second laptop. *It's a place to stay and be near Will.*

And it hit me for the first time just how little I knew about the cowboy I'd attached myself to for the past week with no thought whatsoever of crossing half the country with him, other than that he'd been the only one in years I'd seen stand up to my brother and walk away, even if he did limp after the fact.

And the way he looked at me like I was the only thing in his world at all worth something.

But now I'd found the place he called home, and I wasn't sure I fit here at all.

Maybe the honeymoon period is officially over.

I mourned the loss of that happy connection the moment I realized, and dived into listening to Eve with my full attention, determined not to sink into the depression that usually overtook me whenever I thought about anything family. *That shroud will not touch me here.* The promise I made to myself that I knew I would break sooner than later, but I made it all the same.

Eventually the screen bleared my eyes. I rubbed at them, peering at a row of figures I thought was meant to be merchandise stock, but it didn't seem to quite match up with one of Eve's other spreadsheets from her online store. No matter what I did, I couldn't make the two reconcile. *This is not my forte.* Knowing I was well out of my depth and conceding I needed help, I raised my head.

"Eve, can you—" I looked at the laptop next to me, but its screen was black and the long bench seat beside me sat empty. "Uh, Eve?" I spoke to the empty room that smelled like roast and garlic and family memories.

Is this how she passes the hours on her own and forgets to be lonely?

I stood and stretched slowly. Something in my back popped and I inhaled a little deeper than I had been able to before. That turned into a yawn as I collected the coffee mugs left on the table and headed to the kitchen, peering around but Eve wasn't anywhere. The whole place smelled heavenly, and I could see why the boys kept coming back year after year if they were fed so well after a hard day's work on a regular basis.

Even with the still warm weather, though I was sure the nights would be chill, a fire was lit in a—matching to the theme of the house—oversized fire-place off to one side of the kitchen where a group of worn leather couches covered with knitted blankets were grouped together in a cozy collection. Chestnut hair draped out from one of the ends.

I opened my mouth to call out, but hands wrapped around my waist, pulling me back into a hard, warm body that smelled of leather, sweat and hours of work under a warm afternoon sun. The only sound that elicited out of my mouth was a soft squeak.

CHAPTER THREE

CASSIE

A callused hand cupped over my lower face, tugging me backwards, until I leaned into a hard frame I was starting to know well.

"Don't wake her," Will murmured. "She works hard, and I don't think she's had any help for a long time. Travis isn't good at any of the stuff she does, and the boys wouldn't have the first clue how to do what she does. Not that boys can't do what she does, but... not these boys, anyway. Eve is...kinda special." Will's voice held a wistful note, and my stomach, that had knotted when he placed his hands on me, plummeted.

"I figured that." I twisted in his hands, batting them away from my white knit. "How dirty are you, cowboy?" The moment the words fell out of my mouth, I heard the invitation in them.

So did Will.

He took a step forward, crowding me against the bench. "You wanna say that again, Cassie?" he asked softly, not relinquishing his grip on my waist. His thumbs slipped beneath my knitted hoodie, tracing over the lace beneath. Warmth met barely covered skin and heat rose in his gaze. "Take this off for me later, before you go to bed." It wasn't a request.

I swallowed. "Alright." My hands rested on his forearms, tracing the corded muscle there. "Is everyone coming in now?"

He didn't move, resting his weight against my body, keeping his voice low. "Not just yet." Those thumbs traced circles over the lace just above my hips. "I wanted to spend a few minutes with you first. It'll cost me some hard work tomorrow, but you're worth it."

His mouth grazed mine before I could think, and then his kiss consumed me.

This was the cowboy I'd been infatuated with for the last week, the one who I'd run away with on the chance of freeing myself from my family and my brother's overpowering reach. The cowboy who placed me before anyone else. For the first time in my life, someone wasn't telling me who I was or what I needed to do, unless it was by my choice to be here.

And he was intoxicating.

Will's mouth slanted over mine, his tongue brushing across my bottom lip, but mine were already parted on an easy sigh, granting him all the permission he would need. And he took that, one hand rising to cup the back of my head as he pressed our bodies closer together. My heart beat faster, my attention scattering as I sank into the sensation of kissing him back. Even on our drive across states we took everything slow. It was like being here brought an edge out in him I hadn't seen since our first night together. Even then we hadn't done more than fool around. Not that we had time before we were interrupted. But this—

Will's kiss was fire, consuming me. A soft breath left me as he squeezed me tight and then drew back, gliding his fingers through my hair.

"Hell, girl. If that's how you kiss a cowboy, I swear I'll do anything to come home to that every night," he rasped.

Dark brown eyes bored into mine as I clung to his shirt. The thought that he was filthy and I was clean struck me, but I didn't try to get away from him. Somehow, none of it mattered. All I wanted was him closer. I fiddled with the top button on his shirt, flicking at the edges.

A soft laugh tore from him. "Cassie." His hand closed around mine, stopping the action. "Don't tease me."

I looked up at him through my lashes, my breaths fast and shallow. "Who's teasing?"

We never talked about sex, and we only ever took it slow. I didn't know why. I got the impression that there was nothing virginal about the cute as sin cowboy who every girl at the rodeo loved because he had the looks and the manners to go with the whole package. Everything, except the money.

Good thing for me, that last part didn't really matter. I figured working for it mattered, and earning from the bottom up mattered. And Will—he worked hard. I might be looking at life from a skewed lens, but even though I came from money, that funding wasn't always as readily available to me as it seemed.

Will's hands flexed on my hips. "If this was our place..." He licked his bottom lip, and I remembered the taste of him on my tongue. "Smaller, yeah?" He grinned, and I knew what he meant. Red Hart was grand. Too grand. This was a place to stay. Not make our own.

I offered him a shy smile as my legs shook a little. What started out as a simple tease—what he called me out on—fast turned into a deeper conversation. "Smaller is good," I whispered. "Smaller is really good."

He watched me carefully. "Even for a rich girl?"

It was the first time he called me out on it. His thumbs never stopped their gentle massage, his touch reassuring. So many things had changed today and I wasn't sure exactly what he was asking.

"I'm not the person you think I am." I offered him instead a truth of my own, if ambiguous, wishing he'd place those addictive lips back on mine. My head swirled with need for him while wanting to walk away from the house and keep talking. Wishing we'd talked this way for the whole week.

What did we do for a week of travel? That's right, we slept, curled in each other's arms, talked of nothing and everything. All the inconsequential stuff. We built trust and for the first time, I felt less like someone's possession, someone's trophy, and just...

Was.

Besides Will, I was just there. And I liked being there with him. That's what I wanted. What I wanted to keep happening. And in one short day, so much of that had changed.

And some of it hadn't.

"Kiss me?" I begged softly. So quiet that I wasn't sure I spoke loud enough or even at all until his mouth covered mine in the sort of kiss that relocated entire mountain ranges in a heartbeat.

His arms wrapped around me, heedless of how filthy he was to my clean clothes, and when he drew back, I was no longer panicked or restless. My breaths came slow and even, and I rested in his arms, my body soft and languid.

"Better?" he asked, stroking my cheeks with both thumbs.

I nodded, not trusting myself to answer.

Voices filled the room, and the figure sleeping under the sofa shifted, yawning and stretching like I had done before Will walked in. A moment before we were alone and then the house was full of rowdy voices and clattering feet. Warm bodies filled the space that echoed minutes before—with my moans, my cheeks steaming to prove the point—as Will kissed me harshly once more and wrapped me against his body.

"Should I be concerned about the longevity of this hoodie?" I mumbled into his arm where I rested my head, watching ranch hands, a few I recognized from our arrival into Red Hart earlier in the day. One or two waved at me and I offered a tentative wave back, looking up at Will.

He watched me, and squeezed my waist. "You don't need my permission for anything, Cassie. Not unless you want it." The squeeze became a pull back against him as his meaning altered a little. I swallowed a nod to let him know I understood. He kissed my temple. "You wanna sit down? I think some of Eve's things are on the table."

"Actually, Cassie has been helping me out all afternoon." Eve appeared magically before us, apparently completely refreshed though even I could see the worry lines that creased her forehead.

Will stiffened behind me, and I knew I wasn't the only one to notice. "Did you? How'd you go?" Curiosity warred with a need to help in his voice, but eventually he leaned back against the bench, though his arms remained tight around my waist.

I didn't mind that one bit.

"I was—"

Terrible. I didn't understand half of it. I can't even work a simple job. My mouth parted on the first part of the confession, but Eve beat me to it.

"She's a natural. Set up an extra spreadsheet, picked up mistakes I haven't been able to see even though something had been bothering me and I knew it wasn't right the whole time. Right, Cassie?" She smiled brightly at me, and it was like standing under a freaking spotlight.

I gaped at her in the same manner as a dying fish that flopped out of a fish tank with no hope of ever regaining water again, the opposite of the fish I drowned once in its own tank.

"Uh— sure?" I said weakly.

"I knew you'd fit right in here." Will pressed his lips to my temple. "I need to help out. Can you grab the laptops and things? There's an office some-where..." He looked around and shrugged like one would appear on demand for him.

"I'll show you." Travis grabbed Eve by the shoulders, guiding her to the table under duress as Jude strode around the kitchen and pulled out a stack of plates. "We've got this."

"What happened to 'my kitchen, my rules'," I asked as an older man with gray shot hair pressed a tumbler of what looked like whiskey into Eve's hand.

"Thanks, Gage," she murmured, shrugging helplessly at me. "I guess they've got it."

"This way." Travis handed me a laptop and charger stack, leading me behind the kitchen, past a second lounge area that overlooked the same view as my room. "When Eve isn't about, feel free to work in here. I share the space, but usually I'm out on the land. Office work isn't my favorite thing, unless I'm forced to do it." He grimaced, and pushed opened a cherrywood door.

The room inside was laid out in paneled wooden walls. A large desk occupied the main space, with several comfy looking chairs placed about it. A few leather bound ledgers sat on one corner., and old volumes with gold lettering filled a bookcase set against one wall.

"Travis, this is..."

"Old, and obsolete, I know." Travis rubbed a hand over the back of his back. "I hate this room."

I shook my head, barely daring to take a step inside. Unlike the rest of the house with its hardwood sassafras flooring, this room was carpeted in a plush wool, so that every foot fall was muffled perfectly. "No, this is stunning," I whispered. "It's the perfect workspace. I know—" I took a deep breath. "I understand why you prefer to be outside. That is also stunning. But this room is glorious, Travis."

He shook his head. "Well, it used to be my father's. For now, it's yours. Share it with Eve. Get what you need done. It will stop her from staying in the damn room of hers, cloistered away."

I frowned. "She hides up there?"

Travis' mouth snapped shut. "Help her anyway you can," he said in a softer voice, though the tension in his shoulders basically left him vibrating.

The ranch owner turned on his heel and left me alone in the opulently appointed room that should have belonged to him, but didn't.

And yet again I was left in a place that should have felt comfortable and luxurious for all its beautiful appointments...

But nothing did.

And just like before, it felt like for all Red Hart Ranch's amazing outlooks that there was something terribly, horribly wrong with this place.

CHAPTER FOUR

WILL

I managed to hold my girl and not ruin the fluffy white thing she wore for the second time in a week, but it was a near thing. My arms ached from the different sort of work than holding onto a bull in the practice yards or praying for my life when the chute opened on the rodeo grounds come showtime.

No, my body ached for all the right reasons

tonight—for the hours of work put in on land I cared about, working for people who mattered to me, and for the girl in my arms who slept alone each night who should be curled around my body come nightfall.

I knew that deep inside me, no matter how ridiculous it sounded, and I'd work my ass to the ground to make sure it happened, even if it broke me in the process. As long as it didn't break *us*.

Those first few days were rocky. I could see the uncertainty rising in Cassie. The new work, being thrown in with a stack of new people all at once. Hell, I could understand it myself. The first season I spent at Red Hart I found the underside of every shithouse job there was. Back then, Jude hadn't quite found his feet as foreman, nor had Travis found his wife, Natalie, who curbed his wilder nature. They were fun times, back when the full Beaumont family ran RHR land. That year I learned a lot. Not least of all how strong a woman could be under duress. My gaze drifted across to where Eve leaned back in her chair, exhaustion clear across her strained face.

I squeezed Cassie's arm, and shifted in my seat. A restless energy slithered through me. It had been present these first few days, typical of a new season, with new hands in place. Sure, there were a few regular faces—trader Kyle was on board for a few weeks. Gage had come through and never left, and a few of the older hands I recognize from previous season's work had returned. There were a few new faces too, and that changed the energy up, in a good way.

But what bothered me was the restless energy that rippled through the bones of Red Hart present in the house, the land itself. It might seem a romanticized notion, but I knew if I talked to Travis about it, or Jude, or any of the older hands, they wouldn't laugh my thoughts off. Every one of us who'd been around the land here for more than a season, lived here for a whole, no matter how long or short, knew that Red Hart land was distinct from any other.

I gripped my beer—the only one I'd allow myself for the night—and downed the end of it, pressing a quick kiss to Cass's temple. "I'll be right back," I murmured, pushing back from her, our plates already in my hands.

"Gonna take ours, too?" Gage watched us from across the table, his arms wrapped around his pregnant wife, Brit.

She threw a sunny smile at me as she curled her body into his, seated between his legs. He'd built her a cabin somewhere on the eastern boundary, last I heard, and I made a note to stay right away from that section from the way he watched her, then dipped his head to kiss her hard.

Light fingers grazed the back of my hand. I sent a tight smile Cassie's way. "I'll be back in a minute," I murmured, holding her gaze and letting her see the promise in my eyes. Somehow I'd find a way to get some time together, but it wouldn't be tonight, or any night soon. Not until I earned myself some grace in Jude's book. That meant a whole lotta solid hours, and maybe a fluke or two of luck while we were out working.

But mostly just keeping my head down and working damn hard.

Cass nodded, nibbling her lip as she watched the couple opposite us, then dragged her gaze away from their obvious show of affection. I knew Gage had his own place, his own set of rules, but Cass and I weren't that set up just yet and I wasn't prepared for her to be on show for all the boys all the time.

And I knew the stories that ran around the bunkhouse about Brit and Gage, and I didn't want those sorts of tales told about my girl. Gage seemed to thrive off it, and that was fine, but it wasn't my style.

"Okay," she mumbled, toying with the hem of her fluffy kitted hoodie thing.

I still hadn't gotten it off her to show the lacy top she wore underneath, and maybe in hindsight, that was a good thing. The urge to run my hands under it and find out how she felt as I kissed her senseless left me swaying where I stood.

Shaking myself out of my stupor, I forced my feet to move away from my girl, around the hands who still lingered in the big house, a few finishing up their drink for the night, some still chatting though most had headed back to the bunk house to turn in for the night. The air was still chill outside, and despite the warmth in the big house, the mountain air stripped away any pretense that winter was nearby just yet.

"She's worried." Gage leaned over the edge of the kitchen bench where I stalled, the stack of plates still in my hands.

I glanced sideways at him, and placed the plates in the sink one at a time. "Who are we talking about here?" I kept my voice low, and tried not to look at Eve.

He turned his beer in his hands, running his thumb across the edge of the label, stopping shy of peeling it off. "Eve," he murmured.

"Which is why your girl is worried," Gage finished for me.

I stared at him, and my gut clenched down on the ample dinner I'd eaten. "What?"

Gage studied the glass bottle then placed it in front of him with precision. "You spend a lot of time worrying about her, Will. Maybe a bit too much. Cassie's new here. She doesn't understand how things run. And she doesn't know what Eve's been through." He lifted a shoulder and dropped it. "Either time."

My blood turned to ice. "You mean—"

"I mean exactly what I say." His tone turned sharp. "And you need to watch your girl and let Eve's man look after her."

"Archer's not here," I snapped back, running my hand through my hair. *He's never here.*

I clamped my mouth shut before I said something I'd regret. I'd been here when a whole lot more than the proverbial shit hit the fan. And I'd been here when Archer promised to come back—and he didn't. The first time, and the second. I understood what, but now all I saw was that the woman we all loved and respected was hurting a whole hell of a lot.

Gage nodded. "No, he's not. And that's her choice to keep chasing him, or let him slide, kid."

My mouth twitched at the nickname. "Sure. And if it was you and Brit? If you weren't here and she needed help? What would you want someone to do?" I was pushing it, and I knew it. No one touched Brit. You could look but you sure as hell didn't cross that line. Those were Gage's rules, and everyone knew them.

The cowboy beside me froze. He took his time answering me. "I think the man who decided that my girl needed help would want to be damn sure that I was in a hospital bed, and that the danger she was in outweighed the danger to himself."

I snorted. "You think anyone helping your wife should be so selfish? Is that the goal?"

"It is if you want to live." Thankfully he dropped the not-endearment this time, but the message came through loud and clear.

"I'll keep that in mind." I ground my teeth. The point he made before rankled, though. "You're saying I'm not taking good enough care of Cass."

Gage considered. That was something I learned last season here, that it took a while to get the answers I needed from the older man who had a good fifteen years on his wife, but that the words that came out were far more often than not well worth the wait.

"I'm saying that you need to consider how she sees Red Hart life, and what she doesn't know about its history. Maybe you want to take her on a tour."

I watched Cass slide her arms across the table and place her head on them, her eyes closing just before she sank down in full onto the table. "You mean, like a date?" No chance was I going to get time out to do that.

Gage shrugged. "Tell Jude you need to take his new social media manager on a field trip around the property for a few days. She needs to know the best vantage points to advertise the property and the herd. You can show her around. He can't argue with that."

I opened my mouth to fight him on it, but he had a point. If Cass was handling the marketing like Eve had asked, then she really did need to know more about Red Hart and I probably did know a bit more about the place than I thought.

"Uh, sure. Thanks."

"Don't mention it. And go give your girl some attention, yeah? She needs a little TLC over there." Gage straightened, dwarfing me and half the house.

"Yeah. Right. Hey," I turned my back to the table, pausing in washing up. "How do you deal with the rumors about you a Brit that rip through the

bunk house? You gotta know that half the boys are—"
I shut my mouth just in time, figuring that Gage probably wasn't the man to fess that little secret up to his face.

He sent me a wry smile. "That the new kids jerk off to the image of me fucking my wife rough against the tree outside the bunkhouse while she screamed for me?" He finished his beer and tossed it into the recycle can. "That one's true, kid. They can jerk off all they fuckin' want to that image, and few other stories gettin' around. We're a pair of filthy fuckers." He sauntered away, leaving me with a red face and a need for my girl in a damn fine hurry.

In the end, I finished washing up alone, and by the time I made it back to Cass, she had sagged into a soft mess opposite Brit who was headed the same way. Gage sent me a hard stare, reminiscent of our earlier conversation as he lifted his pregnant wife easily and carried her bridal style out the door of the big house, covering her in her jacket and sliding her boots on without ever putting her down.

"There's goals right there," I muttered as I slid in beside Cassie.

Her hair tumbled over her face and I stroked it back, casting a quick glance Eve's way. Worry lines crossed her forehead even in her sleep. My heart clenched down as I watched Travis shift her gently in her seat, something her mother used to do for Len, their father. Used to, because we lost them both in short order.

When I returned my gaze to Cassie, still stroking her hair absently, I found her blue eyes that I swore missed nothing fixed on me. *Busted.* I swallowed guiltily but didn't stop stroking her hair.

"Hey," I murmured. "I wanna take you up to bed, but I'm not allowed. Will you let me hold you for a while, if you're not too tired?"

She studied me for a minute, then nodded, sliding into the space I made, opening my arms for her. The warmth of her seeped bone deep into me. I leaned back, gathering her into me. My shoulder ached, taking her weight, but I didn't care. The rest of me didn't hurt an ounce, finally holding her the way I wanted.

"I wish we could sleep together," I murmured, exhaling in a blast when he stiffed a fraction against me. "Not—anything specific. Just, sleep. You and me, curled around each other like we did on the drive here. Do you remember?" She made a non committal noise. *Gage was right. I've left her alone for too long, thinking she was alright.* I kept stroking her hair, kept talking even though we were both on the cusp of exhaustion. "Falling asleep on those shitty mattresses, the ones in the highway motels where once we climbed into bed together, we kinda rolled into the middle and couldn't get out of the bed again. Remember those?"

She laughed at my chest. Just a puff of warm air, but it was enough to fracture the tension. "I remember the place we called the Wobbly Boot. It had that giant shoe on the sign. I don't know what it was supposed to be. The foam was so bad to sleep on. And the neighbors yelled when they weren't, um—"

"Yeah. Um." I grinned reminiscently.

The room next to us might have been rented by the hour. I'd been horrified at the time, prepared to move, but were both shattered and so we stuck it out, listening with a sort of horrified fascination to the symphony of fake moans that ran through the usually quiet hours while we were stuck in our truly terrible mattress.

"The next one was better. It was quiet, at least. No hot water." Cass shivered, pressing her body tighter to mine.

"I mean, if this is the reaction I get from you..." I trailed a hand along her spine and pressed my lips to her ear. "I still want to see this lace top of yours, honey. And you did promise me."

She shivered again, a ripple that trembled her from shoulder to fingertip in the delicious sort of anticipation that left me semi hard in my jeans.

Hold that thought, honey. We couldn't get too carried away at the table, but also, I wanted her so damn bad that I'd be lucky to last a handful of seconds at this rate for her.

"Are you ready for bed? I can't take you up," I said regretfully.

Cassie straightened, sitting up. Her body pressed against mine. "Maybe we can find a way to spend some time together in the morning?" she suggested. "I can get up early."

"I'd like that."

I tipped her head back and grazed my mouth across hers in a barely there kiss that said nothing of what I wanted to do to her. The room was still occupied, and I knew the talk in the bunkhouse. I'd prefer it to be about me not getting any than what the boys all wanted to do to Cass—not that I'd never be able to stop that if they started—and refused to add fuel to the rumor mill fire.

"Please," she whispered to me.

My resolve held firm—just—as I pressed my

mouth to hers, drinking in the sugar violets and coffee scent of her that had been desert.

"Soon," I promised. "Get some sleep, and I'll talk to Jude, alright, honey?"

Cassie nodded, standing up. At this height, my lips were at the perfect height to reach her bellybutton, if I wanted to lean in and kiss her.

A teasing smile played at the corners of her lips. Damnit, I knew that smile, it usually meant she was going to do something that would get me—or her—or get us into a whole lot of trouble.

"Cass," I muttered. "This is where I'm gonna hope you'll be good for me..."

The words barely left my mouth before she grasped the hem of her knitted top thing and yanked it over her head.

And then all I saw was lace, and flesh.

Because that lace top thing underneath the fluffy white thing?

Yeah. It really wasn't a top at all.

And I was damn glad that half the boys had left for the night. Because the lace top? It didn't conceal anything at all. Long sleeved it might be, the deep V-neck enhanced every curve on her body, from the swell over her shoulders to the curve at her waist. And it sure as hell showed the black bra beneath because the lace was as see through as it came.

"Fuck, Cass," I cursed softly.

Reverently.

Hell, I wanted to get down on my knees and worship. Just like every man left in the ranch house.

So much for not setting off the rumor mill tonight.

Cass left me speechless as she walked away with a small, secret smile and blew me a kiss before she headed up the stairs I wasn't allowed to use, and walked away from me for the night.

It was probably for the best. After that show, I wouldn't have lasted any longer with her than I did on a bull.

And my best time on one of those damn things was two seconds.

CHAPTER FIVE

WILL

It didn't take long to settle into a routine of eat-work-sleep-repeat that my body remembered in true Red Hart fashion, nor did it take long for the comments to start in the bunk house. Without Gage present—he had carved himself a place of his own out somewhere beyond the back field and walked in each morning, it was tough laughing off the constant barrage that targeted my girl and what wasn't happening between us.

Jude often was the first out in the mornings, or last in at night. I carried the weight of the comments alone with my usual grin that faded the moment the lights went out and my smile slipped. I couldn't even bring myself to draw my hand to my cock when the memory of Cassie's mouth on mine slipped through my mind, the touch of her tongue, soft and hot and wet still so fresh.

Hell, I could barely think for the excess company I couldn't help but share a living space with. Maybe Gage had it right, but I had a hell of a lot of saving up to do in order to get to where he and Brit were right now. Not to mention the ex-soldier turned cowboy had a good twenty years on me in terms of both life experience and savings.

My shoulder twinged as I collected my kit of drenching equipment. I thought I'd be helping Travis with worming the deer herd for parasites, but apparently I'd been sent out to head up the operation this time around. Usually I helped out. This time, the onus was on me to get it right.

I stood in the barn yard, surrounded by a squad of first timer ranch hands who wore far too clean shirts and cheap boots that wouldn't last the season—

if they were lucky at best, but probably couldn't afford much better—and a small group of deer who snuffled curiously at my jeans.

Pushing gently at a white male fawn who had attached himself to me earlier in the week, I started my run down on the procedure that I'd been giving myself a pep talk on while I gathered my kit from the barn, but the little guy insisted on coming back. Not that I minded too much, but right now he'd end up being my guinea pig if he kept on bumming my hand and checking for snacks if he remained within reaching range.

"Not now, Snowball," I muttered when the fawn nudged me yet again. "Alright. Are you ready?" A few murmurs that didn't convince themselves, let alone me, rang around the group in a muted wave. "I want to get this done before the week's end, and the herd is bigger than you think. We'll have to roundup the remainder from the top end later on, but right now let's concentrate on getting this group done to start with." I grabbed a bucket of feed and led the small herd segment into the crush without looking back. The fawn followed me and that seemed to lead a mini migration.

"Looks like you're up, little man," I muttered. "Sorry about this." We got started, and I learned names of the new hands—Noah, Luke, Reggie, and Whalan—as we went. The work went faster than I expected and we busted through the first small herd and moved onto the next before lunch.

I stepped back after round two, stinking of deer scent, chemicals I couldn't pronounce, spit and who knew what else, but proud of what we had started to achieve.

"Still a long way to go," Gage murmured from where he banged a gate together, starting to set up for Red Hart's apparently impromptu rodeo in the coming week.

I leaned my shoulders against a nearby fence post, using the upright wooden edge to scratch my spine without removing my gloves. "Yeah, they're getting the hang of it, but we're doing okay."

"How are you holding up without her?" Gage never stopped working as he talked, a skill some of the younger men hadn't yet acquired.

I shrugged when he nudged a cooler box my way. So much for not taking the gloves off. I stuffed them into my back pocket, and guzzled water. "Hell. That's all it is. Nothing more."

"Yeah? You want space of your own yet?" He flipped a large metal panel like it weighed nothing at all and slammed it into place, jiggling the whole enclosure.

I grabbed it all before the lot toppled over on him. *That's exactly what I want.* But I wasn't saying that. "Sure. I'd love a place of my own sometime. And a steady job. Then a divorce because staying in one place leaves my feet itchy." *Lie.* I could imagine settling down for Cassie just fine. Anywhere she liked, as long as it wasn't in the middle of a city, and I was with her.

Actually, screw that. As long as I was with her, I'd make it work.

"Uh huh. Get that other gate—yeah, that one." We worked in silence for a while as I helped him out on my break for a bit. Gage didn't stop but I knew he was turning it all over in his head, working out what he wanted to say. "If she's worth waiting for, then she's worth it," he said finally. "You have to make that choice, kid."

The old nickname that usually stung fit the situation too well. I did feel like a kid, well out of my depth in every possible way. I didn't know how to care for myself, let alone for a girl who wasn't out of college yet and grew up expecting a certain level of extravagance that I'd never be able to provide her, regardless of how many bulls I stayed on until the bell or not.

"Might not be my choice to make," I muttered, staring down at hands already scarred and chapped from work at the ranch and rodeos around the country.

Who the hell was I kidding? I had a beat up truck that took my five solid years to save up and buy for myself. No trailer, no place to live. I slept out of bunk houses and in borrowed beds. The only money I had left I'd spent on motels on the drive here, trying to look after the only girl I'd cared about for more than one night. I didn't do anything to my name to show for my twenty five years more than a handful of hard earned calluses and another day's promised work come sunrise tomorrow.

"Are you gonna look like that all day, or are you going to get some work done?" Jude's raspy voice brought my head up and me out of my self-imposed sulk in less than a heartbeat.

"No, sir." I yanked my gloves back on in record time. "Got the first part of the herd done that you left me, and we're ready to roundup the next."

I waved toward the boys milling around behind me, wasted and shaded as well as the herd. Both were bound to cause trouble, the younger ranch hands more if I didn't get them working again soon. I knew that would have been what my crew did a few years back, and this group didn't appear so dissimilar.

Shit, I left them on their own for too long. I officially needed a WWJD bracelet —the *JD* part had nothing to do with our maker, and a whole lot more with the man who'd put a boot up my ass if I didn't move it in short order.

"You've done that, huh?" Jude didn't bother to conceal the surprise in his voice. He cast a sideways glance at Gage, who lifted his next fence panel. "Does he do a good job?"

"Decent." Gage placed the panel down and kicked the next one in my direction so it fell toward me. I caught it with both hands, realizing how not light the damn thing was. "You fuckers gonna help, or just stand and watch me work on my lonesome?"

"Yeah, right." I grabbed the next panel and pinned it in place, with Jude's steadying hand. Then their chatter clicked into place. "Wait, you left me with a babysitter?"

Gage leaned over the railing he just set up and fixed me with a hard stare. "He left you with a watch dog to make sure that you didn't get in over your head on your first time out, didn't fuck up and to make sure you get the kudos when it's due, alright?"

My jaw set, but I held his unflinching gaze in a way that me of two seasons ago wouldn't have been able to, still unsure if I just got handed a load of deer shit or a complement covered in the stuff. "Alright."

"Good." Gage put his head down and kept working.

I glanced at Jude, knowing better than to look for praise from the usually silent foreman. "Which part of the herd do you want me to start on next?"

Long shadows followed me by the time we finished the next roundup. Snowball insisted on hovering around my ankles.

"You're not gonna leave me alone, are ya?" I reached down to pet the lil guy's head. He scampered off like I'd committed the worst crime in the world, daring to touch him. Apparently our relationship was a one way door. Who knew? But my shadow left me while I packed some of my kit for the day, at least.

"Not bad, kid." Gage hammered nails into fence posts I swore he'd done earlier in the week.

I sighed. "Shadow one, meets shadow number two."

He grinned at me from beneath his hat. "Did you think we'd cut you loose and let you roam free around the ranch with your own little team of misfits?"

"The thought had crossed my mind." To be fair, I'd been kind of unsettled at the thought of running my own team alone with no pep talk from Jude or a word from Travis at daybreak, and now I knew why. "Am I getting shipped out tomorrow?"

"Maybe tonight." Gage tossed me a cup of parrot clips. "Hold the top wire for me? Someone managed to cut this earlier with a misfire of clippers. Don't ask," he groused, throwing a dirty look over his shoulder at where a group of ranch hands I didn't know well roughhoused in the dirt behind him. "Even if you think you know what you're doing, most of the time you don't. I'll have words later, when I'm not ready to hand him his ass. But if shit like this happens again, he won't get an invite back next season."

"Who was it?"

"Jackson. In the white shirt."

I winced. "No one wears a white shirt on a ranch." I looped the parrot clasp around the wires while Gage clamped them together. "How far are we doing? Ah, fuck." I shook my head as he pointed well along the yard and up the drive. "Man, I was done for the day."

"Not anymore."

We worked in silence until the big house's door clanged and Eve walked off the veranda with Cassie, both of them lost in their chatter. I stopped working, my arms looped over the railing as I watched Cassie walk beside Eve. Her pale blonde hair drifted about her shoulders in untamed curls, and she wore the same white tank and blue jeans I met her in that night at the rodeo only weeks ago that seemed like a goddam age back.

And I was still a sucker for that look.

One of the boys wolves whistled behind us, and I stiffened.

"Who?" I asked in a low voice.

Gage barely gave the group a glance. "Kid in a red shirt. Still clean."

I suppressed a groan. "Reggie. He didn't put in that much work today. Not like the rest."

"Noted."

Another whistle went up.

"Fuckin' hell." My back straightened. I placed the parrot clips on the nearest fence post. "Jude about?"

"Nah, he went inside." Gage stopped working and looked at me with interest.

"Hey cutie, got some play time? We're done for the day."

Both Cassie and Eve paused, but neither of them turned around, though Eve's shoulders hunched a little deeper.

I placed my hat on the fence post too. "Mind that for me?" Gage nodded. I walked away, and turned back. "And the only person you call *kid* is me."

"Got it."

His gaze weighed on me as I headed over to the group of ranch hands I'd worked with all day, but my assessment remained true. Every one of us was covered in deer crud, except for Reggie who managed to remain almost pristine. The boy from the south—just how far south, he wouldn't say—seemed to have perfect, black curls that hung in ringlets untainted by the same sweat and grit that coated the rest of us head to toe.

A muted pall hung over the boys the moment I stepped forward. Some part of me recognized that pensive air, similar to the one Jude's presence often induced. I didn't know what my face looked like, but if it matched my mood, maybe they had reason to shut the hell up right now.

"Reggie." I stood before the red shirted ranch hand. He looked me up and down, sizing me up, which was an interesting experience as he stood a good head taller than me. Interesting for me, too, as I knew I outweighed him in both bulk and muscle, and I that this wouldn't take long. I doubted he'd thrown a punch outside a gym in his life, if he'd even done that, and I suspected that was where this engagement was headed. Reggie liked to talk big, and act bigger, but on the inside he seemed to be fairly empty.

I could deal with that because whatever happened here, I'd have to wear the consequences of it for the rest of the season.

"You like how the girls look, huh?" I raked my fingers through my hair. Grit and who knew what the hell stuck to my fingers. I'd need one hell of a shower before I went into the big house for dinner for the night. All of us would.

Well, maybe not Reggie.

"Yeah. They look good." Reggie gave me a smile I wouldn't give my grandmother if she still spoke to me.

I nodded, turning sideways to the group. Watching the girls was all too easy. Brit wandered up, her hands wrapped around her belly protectively as they chattered together. My gaze was drawn to Cassie, but I had to admit we were blessed, all of us.

Focusing on what I needed to achieve, I tipped my head to one side. "You know she's taken, right?" I said softly as the boys watched me, watching the girls.

"Which one?" Reggie's voice was too loud in the forced silence.

Three heads turned our way, though I didn't miss Gage's shoulders shaking as he laughed silently. Kept his head down and didn't interfere, though. I filed that away for later, too.

"All of them." I held up a hand and turned back to face him. "I don't give a shit if you can see that Eve's got a man here or not. You don't touch those women, and you don't talk about them. In any way. Don't even fucking dream about them. Not about Cassie, and sure as hell not about Miss Eve. Is that understood?"

"Yeah?" Reggie straightened, towering over me. "What about the fat one?"

I smiled at him. Looked like it wasn't my fight to be had after all. "I mean, I'd tell you, but that would spoil the fun." I stepped back as Gage strode between us, gripped Reggie's arm and hauled him toward the barn to a symphony of the younger man's protests. A moment later they disappeared and the protests turned to muted thumps and groans with only us and the shadows as witnesses.

Letting what they didn't see sink in, I lifted my head after a minute. "Keep your words and thoughts respectful toward Cassie and Miss Eve while you're here and you'll have work next year. If not... you won't be here next week when the truck heads back into White Cap, and your day is gonna be real shit come tomorrow. Understood?" My voice cracked across the yard, soft but clear and I knew it wasn't just the boys before me who heard them.

The thumps from the barn stopped as Gage reappeared.

"What about Brit?" Luke asked in a muted voice, sneaking a sideways glance at the other blonde bombshell in the yard who glowed at the older cowboy as he walked straight at her and claimed a deep kiss.

I stared at Luke in exasperation. *For fuck's sake.* "Did you want to shorten your lifespan by half? Gage's business is his own. If you want to pick a fight with a veteran, you're welcome to it. I don't recommend that course of action."

Shaking my head at the excess of testosterone, I made a mental note to ensure Jude brought in plenty of buckle bunnies for the boys to play around with for the rodeo. This lot were randier by far than I swore I had ever been.

"Fair enough," someone, I wasn't sure who, muttered to my back.

I walked back to the fence post where I left my hat, noting the failing light. Letting out a sigh, I picked up Gage's tools and stowed them in his bag, hefting it over my shoulder. It occurred belatedly that I hadn't given instructions to pack up the rest of *my* things, and I turned back expecting to find the yard still in a mess. To my surprise, Noah, Luke and Whalan and a somewhat dusty and bruised looking Reggie stood with my kit completely packed up, the drenching equipment nowhere to be seen.

"All stowed away, boss," Noah said quietly, offering me a nod.

I raised both eyebrows. That was something new.

"Good job. Hit the showers and clean up before you go in for dinner." I shut my mouth before I said anything else.

The boys filed past me, but their heads didn't

hang, and I took that as a decent sign I hadn't taken my first day on my new job too badly, even if I wasn't sure what the new job was exactly.

All I wanted right now was to clean up, find Cassie. One of those things happened after a lukewarm shower—I was last in line and the hot water didn't last quite that long.

Sitting in the house yard right beside my rusty pick up, making it look more ancient than ever, was a shiny black truck bigger than anything else around, even Eve's stunning white and red branded vehicle.

I sighed and took the steps to the big house two at a time and prepared myself for a really bad night, my shoulder twining with every step. Because the owner of that black pick up did the damage to it last time I saw him, and he'd be sitting with Cass, seeing as he was her brother.

Austin the Asshole had arrived.

CHAPTER SIX

CASSIE

I sat beneath my brother's shadow and tried not to flinch every time his booming laugh overrode the conversation. Jude and Gage watched him with identical expressionless faces, though Travis didn't bother to hide his dislike. And Will...

Will was nowhere to be seen when I needed him most.

I shrugged out from under the arm that Austin threw around me again the moment I freed myself. Forcing a smile I didn't feel, I grabbed his mostly finished beer and waggled it in the air, pantomiming getting him another. My brother's beefy arm finally released me. I staggered slightly under my own weight, bereft of the excess pressure that had held me down through dinner.

Jude rose as I moved away from the table, pausing in the middle of the room for a moment, away from everyone. Here, the chatter wasn't quite as loud and I could hear myself think. Or, not think.

"Are you okay?" He liberated the beers, gesturing me over to the kitchen, walking around the long end of the bench and dove into the oversized refrigerator.

Everything in the big house was oversized, I swore, just to live up to its name and not just in the interest of storage.

"Yes. No. I—" I sucked in a long breath and caught the briefest scent of leather and soap, tinged with pine that I associated with Will, but when I looked around, I couldn't spot him at the table. Disappointment washed over me as I turned back to face Jude and found him watching me with a far too keen eye. "I'm fine. I just thought I'd have more than a few weeks without my brother turning up on my—your—doorstep, is all," I corrected myself.

Jude uncapped two fresh beers and placed them in front of me. "It must be nice to get away from your family at college, halfway across the country."

I stared. "I am— I mean, I'm not—" I closed my mouth and tried again. "What did Will tell you?"

"Nothing I didn't already figure out for myself." Jude started washing plates that Travis brought to him. I held out my hand for the tea towel, prepared to do my bit and wipe up, but the boys both ignored me. "He's not so different, you know, from my story. Left home at fifteen, haven't been back or spoken to the parents since. Don't think the door wouldn't be locked, actually." he gave a hollow laugh and I didn't think we were talking about Will any more.

"I'm sorry," I whispered.

Jude watched me as he cleaned. "I found family here, Cassie. A home, too. Will has friends in lots of places. The rodeo here... he comes back every season. Always welcome. That's the kind of man he's grown up to become." Those gray eyes settled on me, hard but not unkind.

I tried not to fidget under their weight. "He's lucky to have found a place," I whispered, horrified when tears prickled the backs of my eyes and I felt like I couldn't turn away or hide.

"Home is wherever you need it to be, Cassie." Trav stopped wiping and placed his stack of plates on the counter. "It doesn't matter if your story is different, or if your brother is the idiot at the table with the loudest voice, telling the stupidest stories. If you fit here, then here is home too."

I didn't know what to say, so I clutched my beers and shrank a bit. Travis was huge, and he'd always seemed so kind. Now he was more than intimidating, and I had no idea how to hide or step away. My gaze shifted to Jude, but the foreman who rarely smiled didn't offer me an out. Suddenly I was desperate for Eve's company, but I hadn't seen her for hours, either.

The silence stretched on, one of those times when I knew it was my turn and I had to fill the void. "I guess I don't feel like I've been here for long enough to fit in." *Anywhere.* "But you're right. Will does. And I'll go back to college soon. And that's a long, long way from here." We hadn't talked about me leaving. Every time the topic started to come up, we both avoided the shift.

Travis leaned over the counter, grasping one of my hands in his much larger ones. "Red Hart can feel like a lot, Cassie. I know, and I used to hide from the fact...hell, I was born here, and I used to hide from that. But Will fits, and so do you. Just because he's not blood doesn't mean he's not family." Travis let go of my hand abruptly, standing up as warmth hit my back in a wave.

Two hands braced the counter either side of me. I let out a little squeak and inhaled a sharp breath.

Soap, leather and fresh pine.

"Will," I breathed as the other boys went back to whatever they'd been doing before. I swore my mind filled with fog whenever Will was around, and ceased all its usual function.

"Are these boys looking after you?" His presence was strong and taut against my back, pressing me against the bench.

I swallowed hard at the tension radiating from him. Jude watched us unflinchingly, while Travis just kept wiping dishes, ignoring the interaction at his side.

"I'm fine," I whispered, my cheeks burning at hosting this conversation anywhere near other people. "It's my brother I was —" I closed my mouth, wishing I hadn't said anything. The last thing I wanted to do was restart the vitriolic rivalry between Will and Austin.

"I saw." Will leaned down, resting his lips against my hair and inhaled. "Damn, you smell good, honey."

"Oh." Nothing else coherent came out for a moment. "I can, uh, get you a—" I glanced at the other side of the kitchen. But it was empty. Well, mostly empty. Eve wandered out of the pantry, her expression unfocussed as she stared at her phone in her hand.

Will dropped a hand to my hip, his hand flexing there in an undeniably intimate squeeze. His lips trailed across the shell of my ear, leaving a tingling sensation in their wake. "Enjoy your night, Cassie. I'll find you later." He pressed a soft kiss to the sensitive spot behind my ear, then his touch and warmth disappeared leaving me staring at the bare kitchen bench and two beers I didn't care about at all.

I'll find you later.

His promise murmured in a low voice settled over me. I shivered, grabbed the beers and deposited them on the table next to my brother, intent on finding Will, but Austin's arm shot out, grabbing for me again.

"I missed you, sis. The van's been empty without you in it," he proclaimed loudly.

Too loudly.

I winced, letting out a huff. "You mean you had to get up and cook your own meals and clean up after yourself," I snarked back, then wished I hadn't.

Austin's face, already red, swelled slightly with the heat that radiated from him as he turned radish colored. Actually, he kind of resembled one, too.

The first sign of his rage, of which both Will and I were intimately acquainted with. The story I hadn't told anyone else was why I picked a university five states away when there was one within an hour's drive from home.

And it has little to do with parent's weekend or study choices.

"What did you say?" Austin said in a low voice that rippled along my spine.

One of the young ranch hands let out a laugh. I didn't know if it was at our conversation or someone else's. I wasn't game to risk diverting my attention from the predator who watched me now. Both Jude and Travis had moved away from the table, and I was left with a group of coyotes I didn't know at all.

I wrapped my arms around myself, and wished I'd left the beers in the kitchen., stayed with will and ran away for the night.

And never come back.

"I didn't say anything," I whispered. "Sorry, Austin."

"Not that she has anything to be sorry about, Right, Cass?" Gage planted himself right next to me, grabbing the spare beet I'd been torturing that I had absolutely zero intention of driving. "This is for me. Darlin?" he threw me a cocky grin that I managed to return in part.

Austin frowned, looking between us. "Cassie?"

"This is Gage. He's married to, uh—" I looked about, but Brit wasn't anywhere in sight. A rarity as she loved the big house dinners and the social aspect of ranch life from what I could tell.

"My wife isn't well tonight. Though I'd give her some peace and come up, make sure everything else ran smoothly. Heard some of the rodeo crew arrived, and that you might need company while Will got them settled in out back." Gage took a large swig from what had to be a warm beer without wincing.

Relief swamped me. So Will hadn't abandoned me after all. He would be back, like he promised. I just had to survive however long with Austin. But that didn't mean I had to stay with my brother, especially if he was in this mood. Maybe he and Gage could become good friends. It looked like the older man was up for the challenge, and I was feeling sassy.

Taking a leaf out of Brit's book, I smiled sweetly. "Austin, why don't you tell everyone about that time the bull threw you less than a second into your ride?" I excused myself while my brother was still spluttering at the table.

Gage gave me a broad wink as I walked away, heading around the kitchen bench in search of Eve. I found her counting out inventory and making a list on her phone.

"Want some help?" I offered.

"I'm good." Eve frowned at her phone. A moment later she tapped the offending device with a frustrated huff and stowed it in her pocket, offering me a broad, fake grin that didn't hide her worry lines. "I think we still have dessert to serve, don't we?"

"Dessert, right." I watched her open cupboard doors and haul out stacks of bowls half her own height before I joined her, grabbing spoons. Bowls that I swore wouldn't actually first inside the fridge emerged filled with perfectly set dark chocolate mousse. "Wait, when did you get time to do this?" I stared at the bowl and gave it a taster poke.

Nothing so much as moved.

"Four this morning?" Eve sent me a guilty

glance. "Archer gets up early and I don't get to speak to him all that often."

I blinked. "You call your boyfriend by his last name?"

Eve's laugh seemed more strained than ever. "Everyone else does. And it was a habit from the last time he was here." Her incessant spooning and bowl passing halted.

Plopping a spoon in a bowl, I turned and looked at her. "And when was that?"

She swallowed and looked at me. "Last Christmas?"

"But you've seen him since then, right?" I'd just met Will. Okay, not just met him, but the weeks we'd been together had flown by already, and I couldn't't imagine being away from him for that long. "You've spent more time together than just on the phone, wherever he is?"

She hesitated. "I went to Texas to see him a few months back. It... was good. Great, even." One hand rose to touch the pendant at her neck. It looked like diamonds spread out in an abstract shape, like stars. "I— we ran into some trouble. But he's coming back," she whispered. "He always said he would." The hand dropped, and she returned to spooning.

And didn't talk again.

I rolled my lips inward. Whoever Archer was, I was already prepared to have words with him. I was sure he had a good reason for not being here, but surely he knew Eve was hurting if he had spoken to her just this morning. And before the sun rose? Who was this guy?

I grabbed some bowls and turned around, running straight into Jude.

"He's a better man than you think. Saved her life more than once."

I bristled at being blindsided by the stocky foreman. "That doesn't mean she owes him," I snapped, then lowered my head. "Sorry. I just— She's not okay."

He nodded. "I know. But she loves him."

And apparently, that was enough. He liberated the bowls in my hands, and walked away. I stared after him, but there was nothing left to say to anyone. My mind whirled. I wanted to rant and rave on her behalf but maybe it wasn't my business. There was obviously a history here I knew absolutely nothing about, and I hadn't been around Red Hart long enough to pry, despite working side by side with Eve most days.

On others, I worked alone in Travis's luxury appointed study. It was quiet there, but it still felt like I invaded his space even though I worked inside it with his permission.

I stared after Jude where he retreated across the open space to the table bearing bowls of mousse, and counted in my head. It didn't take more than a handful of seconds before the mass of ranch hands figured out there was more food on offer. They swamped the kitchen—bearing their best manners, of course, for Eve under Travis's watchful and somewhat grumpy eye. I didn't think I was alone in noticing her mood, but her twin seemed to have everything under control for now.

Stepping back, I bumped into a warm body. Hands clasped my hips as a smile spread over my face and my heart lurched. *Will*.

CHAPTER SEVEN

CASS

Hope warmed my cheeks as I glanced back, only to be assailed by a gust of beer breath. Panic slapped me in the face as I realized another man had his hands on me, and not the one I wanted to hit on me.

Reggie, one of the hands who I thought worked with Will, grinned down at me. One palm rested on my hip as he reached around me for a bowl. "Why don' t you sit with us, darlin'?" he purred, putting on an accent I swore he stole straight from Gage. "I'm sure we could use some company from someone as pretty as you."

A sidestep got me out of it, but I swore I'd feel his touch until I scrubbed my skin with hot water and maybe bleach. Pursing my lips into something akin to a smile even though it was fake as hell, I glanced over his shoulder and spotted—

My brother.

Welp, in times of need, one must do what one must.

"Sorry. Got a hot date." I winked and slipped around the taller man, scooped up a bowl and placed it in Austin's hands. "Save me," I muttered. "I hate being touched."

Austin, predictably, launched an arm around my shoulders. Not what I wanted but his bulky embrace provided a barrier between me and the rest of the crowd. "Come on, Cass. Lemme tell you what I've been up to while you've been away."

I wanted to punch the ego that inflated around him on sight, but since I needed his intervention, I held that impulse back. "Sure, big guy. Let's do that," I said, letting out a sigh.

Austin talked all the way back to the table, all the

way through his dessert and halfway through the rest of the boys leaving. I didn't listen to a word, putting in a nod when I thought I was supposed to, and made a few positive noises of support. They were the same stories I'd heard before, after all, just different versions.

Ausitn rode the bull, wowed the crowd, and got laid.

Austin won the trophy, downed the yard glass and danced all night and ... yup, he got laid. (I didn't need the details that followed, so I vagued out, though from the cheer that went up around the table, he told the story quite well).

Austin saved a cow from danger after interpreting its frantic mood and saved the day. He probably got laid then too.

Okay, so I made that last one up. Actually, I'd never seen him *get* laid—thankfully—because he never brought any of the women he claimed to discover back to the trailer we had shared for several rounds of the rodeo circuit, and for that I was eternally grateful. I didn't know how many of my brother's stories were true or not, but the more he ate, drank and got rowdy with the ranch hands, entertaining them with endless stories as the night wore on until they frittered away for the next day's work, the darker and more closed Jude and Trav's faces became.

Eventually, I pulled away from him, intent on heading upstairs and turning in myself.

So much for I'll find you later.

I closed my eyes and drew in a fortifying breath, certain I'd have a fight on my hands with Austin when I opened them. He was never one to hit the hay early, especially when he thought there was at least one member of the audience left to regale, whether they wanted to hear more fake *Austin saved the cow* stories or not. A wave of leather and soap scent washed over me. I opened my eyes to find Will striding across the room, headed in our direction. His eyes were dark, and the curls I loved to wind around my fingers fell across his darkened eyes. He made no effort to push them back as he usually did when he reached our table, nor did he stop walking until he reached my side and held out his hand.

"Come on," was all he said, without a glance at my brother.

Austin stopped mid-story, looking disjointedly at Will like he only just realized the man I left him with at the last rodeo was here. "What are you doing," he started.

I didn't give my brother a chance to finish.

"Goodnight, Austin," I murmured, scooting forward off the bench seat as I placed my hand into Will's.

Roughened fingers closed around mine in a firm grip as he drew me forward, away from Austin. Warmth traveled along my arm as he strode away from the table, heading toward the front door of the big house. I kept pace, my legs working quickly as I shifted out of my semi-dozy state of the night. Will seemed to have a singular focus. Warmth spread between us where his skin contacted mine. I felt eyes on us as we crossed the living area, but no one said goodnight or stopped us. My heart pounded in my chest as he pushed open the door and paused long enough for me to push my boots on, but when I grabbed for my coat, he caught my wrist and shook his head.

"You won't need it," Will said in a low voice. His eyes were so dark in the shadows I couldn't read his intent.

"It's cold out," I said nervously, tugging at the lace sleeves of my top where his hand closed around my wrist.

"I'll keep you warm," he promised, sliding his hand down around mine, and pulled me off the veranda.

I tripped down the steps after him, my objection half stuck in my throat, lodged halfway between my heart and my curiosity. Will rounded the corner of the big house, stepping into the shadows. Darkness engulfed us a moment later, as we moved from the noise and the warmth and laughter inside the house. It wasn't the only thing—a shiver worked its way across my shoulders as the night's cold tendrils reached out in an intimate caress. I pulled my hand free of Will's wrapping my arms around myself as he stopped, staring up at the mountain behind the house.

"Will, it's freezing," I whispered. The contrast of the warmth from inside the house and the chill air, heralding winter's brisk call was all too evident as gooseflesh followed my shiver in a full body ripple.

"Come here." Warmth engulfed me again as Will's arms slid around me. His jacket wrapped around my back as he tucked me into his chest and angled my chin up. "It took me too long to get back. I wanted a chance to make that up to you."

I started to say that it didn't matter, but that would have been a lie. Beside Austin I'd been uncomfortable since the start of the night and wanted to hide in Will's arms the entire time. Call me needy or whatever, but tonight was the night that I really had needed him.

And now he was here, smelling like all over leather and soap with freshly washed hair that fell over his eyes in soft curls. I reached up to brush his curls back, but he trapped my hands between us, lowering his mouth to mine.

"Don't move, just for a minute," he murmured. His voice was low and lazy, like he savored the moment.

I nodded, and then his mouth was on mine, his lips moving in a slow pressure that left me inhaling sharply. Glad he pressed me tight to him, I knotted my hands in his shirt, holding his closer.

"*Don'tletmego,*" I mumbled against his mouth.

Will made an amused huff and swept his tongue across my bottom lip. Tingles raced through me as I gasped softly. The hands around me tightened, pulling me closer as he drove his tongue inside my mouth, and shifted us backwards. The cold surface of the house hit my back through my lace top as his kiss grew intense, the tips of our tongues touching, then so much more. Rougher. All I could think about was trying to match his fervor, but I could barely concentrate enough to kiss him back. A knee slid between my legs as he pressed his body to mine, pinning me against the wall. Sensation flared through me with every tiny shift, leaving me beyond flustered, kneading his chest lightly with my nails. I couldn't move, and I didn't want to. Will hadn't seemed that dominant before but now...

Will's tongue drove into my mouth relentlessly, removing the need to think. I moaned, arching against his touches that left me aching in all the right/wrong places. His hands travelled along my back, warmth searing through me from both sides as his jacket draped around both of us. I pressed up to kiss him back and found my moan muffled by his deep kisses that left me needier than ever.

And breathless.

I inhaled the scent of him, knowing I'd want to sleep in this shift to keep that fragment of him near me. As though reading my mind, one hand wound between us to cup my breast through my bra, squeezing gently as he traced over my nipple. I let out a startled gasp. Pleasure rippled through me as I pressed my breast into his hand and swore he laughed into my mouth at the action. My moan as I ached did little to alleviate the need tearing through me. I needed to be closer to him. I needed these damn clothes off.

I needed—

"Whoa, honey. Slow down," Will drew back from our kiss, his lips gliding across mine as he spoke. "You gonna let me taste you tonight?"

I frowned. "You just did."

He huffed a breath against my lips as his thumb traced across my waist band. "You sweet mouth, yeah, honey. I know what that tastes like. I want to lick you here." His hand dropped between my legs, rubbing the seam of my jeans with two fingers.

I moaned at the riot sensation that overwhelmed me, knowing he'd be able to feel the heat emanating through the stretchy denim, how needy I was from just his kisses and a few touches.

"You want me to taste you, Cassie?" he murmured across my lips, flicking at the button to my jeans.

I couldn't answer, could barely think. "Here?" I shivered again as he stepped back, looking me over.

"Fuck, I want you so damn bad." One hand wrapped around my nape and pulled me forward, until our mouths crashed together again.

I left him in no illusions that this was what I wanted too. "Please," I gasped as his hand pushed down the front of my jeans.

A high laugh that came from neither of us, and

the deep, highly recognizable voice of Gage who answered his wife emanated from around the corner.

"Damnit." Will claimed my mouth one more. "Maybe that's a good thing." He stroked my stomach gently.

"Never a good thing." I rubbed my cheek against his stubble. "What about my needs?"

He shifted his knee back between my legs. "I thought we saw those, honey?"

"Did we?" I assessed him, managing to cover my gasp.

Will's eyes darkened as he braced his body over mine, pushing his knee up between my legs as he had before. This time his hands rested on my hips. And he smiled. "Ride me."

Heat flushed my cheeks and I shook my head, tucking my chin to hide from him, but we both knew I couldn't get away. He laughed again, that same soft sound that I knew wouldn't make it any further than either of us, that left my heart happening in my chest. Will pressed me back against the house, his knee high between my legs so I couldn't move and rested my tip toes.

"You wanna go back inside, you come for me right damn wow. I wanna see you fall apart."

"Why?" Of all things, that was what slipped out.

Will looked at me like I was crazy. I didn't blame him.

"Because you're mine, and seeing you flushed and messy and all the things you're not supposed to be is sexy as fuck, honey." He leaned down to kiss my mouth as I whimpered. Apparently, that was enough.

His knee pressed harder, until I leaned my head forward, gasping into Will's shirt.

"Too good," I managed, between breaths.

"Hold them," he commanded. "Don't breathe out or in." I sucked in a breath and rocked my hips on his leg, arching up for a kiss, and found his hands solid in their grip. "I wanna hear you moan," he encouraged me.

I glanced sideways to where I knew Brit and Gage played a similar game from her soft sighs and occasional smart remarks, punctuated by Gage's deeper laughs.

"I don't think I—*oh*," I whispered, as Will leaned in impossibly, his body filling all the spaces I thought were already oppressed to mine.

"Yeah?" His mouth grazed mine in a not quite kiss as heat deluged my thighs. "That sort of *oh*, honey?"

Will's tongue traced my bottom lip lazily as I

shivered, rocking my hips over his thigh. He felt so good and I knew we shouldn't be out here, when everyone was inside, including Jude and Travis and my brother, and—

"I can hear you thinking, Cassie." Will's deep voice filtered through my world as he spoke into my ear. His lips framed the delicate shape leaving me extra shivery. "You think they know you're out here with me, all hot and bothered and aching? Think they know that if I slide my hand inside your panties you'd be dripping for me, all ready for me to slide inside you and—"

He didn't need to finish, because I did first.

I came for him with a cry he muffled with his mouth, thrusting his tongue deep inside to steal my scream. I rocked my hips over his thigh where he pinned me between the warmth of his hard body and the unyielding house wall, riding out the waves of pleasure brought on by his teasing and filthy words.

As the wave of sensation subsided, he let me collapse into his arms, holding me tight. "Christ, you're beautiful." Will wove his hands through my hair, kissing me hard, then slower, taking his time. I sank deep against his chest, resting my head there. His kisses weren't sweet and gentle anymore. Something had changed between us, some knowledge that this was our new normal and that we'd ramped it up a little. "I wanna take you somewhere tomorrow. Bring the camera Eve has for the property, okay? I'll be here early."

I smiled against his shirt. Knowing Will, early meant well before dawn, but the thought of spending time with him left me more boneless than ever.

"Alright." I rubbed my cheek against his chest. "I want to stay here with you."

Brit's laugh turned into a different sort of sound, and I wondered how loud I'd been a moment before. Gage muttered something. I couldn't hear his voice that was deeper than ever, and Will cursed softly.

"I think our time is up, Cass." He stared down at me with dark eyes. "Come back inside. I'll take you up."

"I thought you weren't supposed to go upstairs?" I let him take my hand against, shivering the moment he stepped away.

"I'm not."

I didn't get to say anything else as he towed me around the front of the house where the last of the ranch hands and newer arrivals were heading down to their accommodation for the night. Several of them waved to Will or called out, but he didn't stop or say more than a word or two. I kicked my boots off when he did, and followed him into the house.

He stopped for a quick word with Travis as the heat of the house enveloped me. My shivers stopped and I headed for the kitchen to help but Travis shook his head.

"Not tonight, Cassie. Looks like you two have some work to do early tomorrow. Head up. I'll fix this. Both of you." He frowned at Eve who shrugged at him and tiredly put one foot in front of the other, leaving him to it alone, her attention buried on her phone.

Will gripped my hand again, his eyes hooded.

"Are you allowed up?" I asked, feeling like a teenager asking for her dad's permission and about to break some monumental unspoken house rule.

He nodded once. "Just for a minute. I can't stay," he rasped, his voice straining.

I bit my lip, my body still a little liquid and humming from what we'd done minutes before. I managed the stairs with only the slightest stumble, but Will was there, his hands on my hips to steady me. Gripping his knuckles tight, I kept going, my breath short as I made it to the landing. The hall had never seemed so long. I looked back, wondering if Will wanted the world's briefest tour of the wide hallway, but his attention was focused on just me.

I stepped back under his intense study, and bumped into the doorframe. "This is me," I whispered.

"Yeah?" One arm braced over my head as he kept moving forward until he towered over me. Will wasn't the tallest cowboy at Red Hart, but compared to my five foot six height with his bulky chest, he seemed pretty solid and imposing to me. A fingertip trailed along my cheek. "You like it here, Cassie?"

"I like being anywhere with you," I breathed the admission as my heart clenched. *Don' t fall for the cowboy who will just move on in a few months. Don't fall for the cowboy...*

But it was too late. Will's liquid brown eyes filled my vision as he dipped his head and claimed my mouth in a long, slow kiss that left me rising onto my toes for more. So much more.

And left me breathless and aching when he drew back a moment later, so much more than a midnight promise in the pensive heartbeat between us.

"I'll see you in the morning, Cass," he murmured, his eyes on my mouth, before he dragged his gaze back to my eyes with an effort that looked like it cost him everything. His eye flickered over my shoulder, into my room before he stepped back a fraction, though his hand dropped to my hip, his thump rubbing my skin where my top had ridden up.

Heavy footsteps and a pointed cough announced Travis' arrival at the top of the stairs.

"Goodnight," I whispered, wishing he could come in and finish what we started down stairs. Or just collapse together, and sleep though until morning in the warmth of each other's bodies, though I knew he wanted—needed—more.

Because so did I.

"Goodnight, Cass," he murmured, squeezing my hip.

Then his touch was gone, along iwht his presence as Will strode away along the hall. Travis said something softly as he passed that froze Will on the top step. He half turned back, but the light didn't quite reach him. All I could see was his silhouette outlined against the muted light from downstairs.

Then he wasn't there at all, and I stood alone on the landing.

CHAPTER EIGHT

Cassie

"Where are we going?" I asked for the fifteenth time this hour in the Red Hart version of *Are we there yet*, but Will just smiled and kept driving up the range.

He'd been the same when I found him already waiting for me before dawn over an hour before when I turned up, dressed to—well, not impress, but for comfort and to, okay, so a *little* bit to impress.

Jeans and boots meant I could tackle most things, but the V-neck white tee I knew he loved sat snug on my hips and clung to every other curve I had, and there were plenty of those. He'd already packed a lunch too, basket and all, rug tucked under one arm and half held out ready to go despite that I set a four a.m alarm and hauled my sleepy behind out of my cozy, snuggly bed to ensure I'd beat him into the big house kitchen after last night's intimacy.

Spoilers: I didn't.

I asked him what our plan for the day was back then, too, but he refused to answer me in the big house just as he held his silence now. His hand wrapped around mine offered a gentle squeeze, and he flicked the volume up on Florida Georgia Line's *Cruise.*

Smiling, I took the hint and leaned back in my seat. "Fine, be secret keeper, then," I muttered, getting my faux grouchy on. I avoided my brother this morning, as well as most everyone else by keeping Will Kirk hours, and that put me in a good mood. Maybe I should take the hint and become an early bird like him. Not that being a seven o'clock riser ever counted as a tardy hours person, but still... at Red Hart, seven labeled me as practically a layabout. The kitchen was empty when I came downstairs each morning, and I got to help clean up after everyone had left. I didn't usually mind, because it left me with a sort of peace before I started work for the day, and the chatter in the yard and fields outside stayed there.

But now that I knew a bit more about Will's hours, I kind of liked them. A sense of sadness washed over me. I'd lose that when I went back to college after myself enforced break and Will went back to...whatever came next for him. I couldn't help wondering if that would be it for us, if he would go one way and I would go mine, and our lives might never collide again.

If our path stopped there.

I squeezed his hand a little tighter, suddenly desperate to make today a memory I could keep forever if it was one of a limited few, unable to open my mouth and ask. Unwilling to be *that* desperate girl who clung to the cowboy who ever stayed anywhere. Because that's who Will Kirk was. He didn't put down roots, and he never stayed with anyone. I got that sense of him from the get go, back in the rodeo that night. He lived a fairly spartan existence even then, sleeping in someone else's trailer, skipping from place to place as the crowds demanded, following the sun. Chasing dreams.

But I also wanted to be the dream he followed. Selfish, I knew and also that he wouldn't change. He wasn't made of the same stuff that made Travis cling to his mountain, or Eve ache for her Texas man. Gage, who found who he loved and settled after a lifetime somewhere else. Jude, the stead forth foreman with his Canadian wife who flitted in and out of his life—they had a unique relationship and I wasn't sure I'd ever be able to spend that long away from someone I loved without falling apart.

Loved.

Oh, shit.

I really had fallen for the cowboy with the liquid brown eyes and the heart of gold.

The rodeo rider with wind beneath his feet who never stayed.

My heart squeezed in my chest as I turned my head to look out the window, withdrawing my hand from Will's strong hold.

And my mouth fell open.

"Where are we?"

"North western boundary." He pulled up, facing my window to the view.

And the view did not do what he showed me. No wonder he insisted I bring Eve's camera with all the lenses. I needed several manuals to understand how the thing operated. Because...

Wow.

If I thought Red Hart was pretty before, and that the mountain was imposing, then I had never understood the concept of beauty until right now. We'd driven around the side of the mountain to reach this place, through the foothills while I was lost in my head. Music played in the background but I couldn't hear the lyrics for the sensory overwhelm before me.

Will gestured to the incredible vista that showcased an outcrop of granite that dropped off at one side from golden grasses and late season wildflowers to a deep sweeping valley that dipped between two mountain ranges. They seemed to cross at the bottom, though I couldn't see in the heavily treed area. Everything was green, spotted with the rare outburst of red or yellow. He let me look at my fill before he continued on. A good thing, because I couldn't speak at all.

"There's a collapsed track that leads up the ridge line to Walker Roan's place. He's a bit of a recluse. Heard a girl got under his skin, drove up there one season a few months back and never left. The forgotten mountain man, yeah?" He laughed softly. "Over that way is the Canadian border. It's a bit further out, but not as far as you'd think. Natalie lives out there, and Jude heads out every so often to see her during the season." He paused on that thought, pensive.

"I can't imagine spending that much time apart," I blurted in the softest way possible, then wished I hadn't. "I mean—"

"I know what you mean." Will didn't give me a chance to fix my mistake, putting his truck into park and was out of the driver's seat before I could say anything else.

Maybe he didn't want to hear it. Not that I'd blame him. The weeks between now and when I returned to college seemed all too short and long at the same time.

I unbuckled my seatbelt with numb fingers, and juggled the camera in my lap, desperate not to break that, too. A case of lenses slipped between my hands but larger ones caught them, closing around mine to steady everything. My breath caught as I stared up into Will's face. I'd been so lost in my panic that I hadn't even heard him open the door or realized he stood right next to me.

"Cassie, it's okay," he murmured, capturing everything and tucking it into a pile on my lap, surrounded by his safe grip. "I 'm not gonna leave you alone. Well, maybe while you study, or until you get sick of me hanging out. But other than that..." His head tipped to one side, he studied me with an otherwise expressionless face, and suddenly I couldn't breathe at all. "I can't think of anything worse than being without you, either."

"But you ride the circuit and work here, and– and—" I blurted, unable to form either a cohesive thought, or finish anything.

"And you have to study." He leaned in and took advantage of the fact my mouth was open, kissing me roughly. When he drew back, softening his touch to a mere brush of lips on lips, I was left with less breath than I started with. "Fuck, I've been aching to do that since I saw you come downstairs in that damn tee and jeans, he grated, swallowing hard.

"I wore it because I remembered you liked it," I said, my lips still tingling. I wanted to touch them, see if they were as swollen as they felt, but my hands were trapped beneath his. I didn't want to pull away from his touch either.

"Damn right I did." He kissed me again, gentler this time, and I managed to breathe afterwards. "You gonna take some pictures of this place so we have proof that today was about more than me taking the girl I'm falling for on a date without anyone else interrupting us?" His gaze sliced through me with unimpeded intent.

"Oh." I couldn't respond to that, didn't have any other words.

He didn't seem to need one, thankfully, as his hands slipped around my hips. Will tugged me forward, lifting me out of his truck while I strangled the camera equipment.

"I have no idea how to work any of this," I admitted, placing all the pieces on the picnic blanket he placed on a flat patch that overlooked everything.

Twenty minutes later, we managed to decipher Eve's handwritten notes on the best lenses for which sorts of shots, though Travis seemed to have crossed out a few and added his own diatribe here and there. I laughed at some, and strained my eyes at others while Will did the honors and set it all up.

"Ta-daa." He proudly presented it to me.

"Looks good," I approved, taking the camera from him, and held it up. "Wow, that's kinda heavy. Okay, so promotional shots. Eve gave me a list..."

I delved into that for the next however long it took. The sun warmed my back as Will sat quietly at my side and by the time I got the hang of clicking away, checking the digital screen and resting the frame, I was sure my legs wouldn't work the next time I tried to use them. Actually, I couldn't feel my feet any more at all.

"I'm sorry. That took a whole lot longer than I expected." I bit my lip. "This probably wasn't how you wanted to spend time with me."

Will shrugged, sending me an easy smile. "I'm with you. That makes me happy, honey."

Butterflies rioted in my stomach as he took the camera from my lowered hands and placed it on the far side of the picnic rug. That same warm hand came back to catch my jaw, turning my head as he angled his mouth over mine. Before our lips touched my eyes were already closed. I sank into his touch, relieved not to have to fight to find time with him at the end of the day when I could barely keep my eyes open.

HIs lips traced the shape of my own, pressing a little firmer. I sighed and let him in, letting him lay me back on the rug, tucking me beneath his body. Out here, there was no one to see us, no one to offend or tell us *no*.

For the first time since we arrived at Red Hart, we were alone and it felt so damn good.

Will eased his thighs between mine, pulling back to break our kiss with a question written across his face. I stretched up, needing him closer, but he shook his head.

"Tell me if this is too much," he murmured, cupping the back of my head and massaging my scalp deep enough to draw a moan from my lips for a different reason than how his weight pressed against me felt. "Tell me to stop any time, Cassie."

"But I don't want you to st–"

His thumb brushed over my lips and settled there, silencing me. "You might change your mind," he whispered. "I don't want to take that choice away from you, now or ever. I want you so damn bad, but that doesn't mean I won't listen to what you want, Cass. Do you understand?"

I nodded, my throat too tight to get the words out. "Kiss me?" I finally managed to blurt.

Will huffed part of a laugh against my mouth. "Yes, ma'am."

His kiss started slow but sensual, his tongue sliding between my lips as he pressed his body against mine in a rhythm I could deny. A hitched gasp tore from me as he pushed my legs apart with his knees, the memory of what we'd done the night before flooding back.

Heat flushed me from where our lisp connected to where he ground against me, sensation zinging between the two points. I ached for him to be rougher, like he'd kissed me before, move fast, pull my shirt off, *something*. But today's version of Will Kirk seemed intent on torturing me with every hour we had left together in slow motion.

A deep moan left me as he found a spot on my hip and ran his thumb down the inside, beneath my jeans.

"Please," I whimpered, uncaring how I sounded. "Will–" I tugged at his shirt as he laughed softly.

"Desperate little thing, aren't you?" he murmured, trailing his lips across my jaw line and over my collar bone. "Can I take this off?" he tugged lightly as the material of my tee with his teeth.

Fuck yes.

"Please," I whispered again, reverted to begging for the smallest thing already. "I need..."

"Need what?" He toyed with the hem of my tee, lifting it up and dipped his head to kiss the curve of my stomach. "Cassie?"

"You," I managed as he tugged the top over my breasts and nipped one through my lace bra. "I need you."

"Where?"

"Inside me." Heat rocketed from between my thighs to my cheeks. I was sure my chest flushed, too. "I ache–"

"Not yet you don't." He cut me off, swirling his tongue around my nipple as he rocked his hips into the cradle of mine. "Not yet."

Then all I could do for a long time was make soft sounds he seemed to like until my soft sounds grew into louder ones. I gripped his hair, winging my fingers through his curls and came, pinned to the ground beneath him as he sucked and flicked on my nipple through the lace of my bra.

And he hadn't even taken my clothes off yet.

"Will," I mumbled as he managed to peel the clothing off that should have been gone a while back. "Why haven't we done this earlier?"

He laughed out loud, unbuttoning his shirt and shucking it off to join mine. I lay on the blanket, my knees pushed wide by his, staring up at his defined abs and the heavy muscle I knew he earned every day working his ass off from before dawn until well after dusk.

And did it again and again and again.

This was not the sort of man who pumped iron or didn't know how to change a tire or do a job. He understood hard work. He'd probably also only wear a suit a handful of times in his life, and he'd never work in an office. But the longer I wanted him, the less those things mattered to me. The girl I'd been before I met Will Kirk, that girl's expectations of this life, that all changed in the last month.

I reached for him, the same question in my eyes that had been in his a few minutes ago. He nodded slowly, leaning forward so I could trace my hands along the hard ridges of muscle that layered his torso. He didn't need to flex or so off like many of the other boys might have done, I suspected. Will just waited patiently while I explored, flinching only once when I touched his shoulder where he'd been hurt a while back.

"Sorry," I murmured as he reached down and flicked the button on my jeans. "It still hurts?"

"Sometimes," was the only answer he offered, intent on peeling the denim from my skin one inch at a time.

Will leaned forward, licking the insides of my thighs. Warmth, then coolness hit my skin as he took my panties with my jeans to my ankles and wiggled them over my feet. "Take your bra off."

I stared. "What, you don't have magic hands for that too?" I challenged him.

His wicked grin was my answer as he pushed my legs apart and knelt between them. Then his tongue was on my flesh, and I didn't fight him any longer. The only problem I had was trying to concentrate while he ran his tongue along my skin until I moaned aloud. My head hung back as I arched, my hands trapped beneath me as I failed to work the clasp on my bra.

"That's a view," he muttered, his breath warm on my clit.

I shivered, pressing my hips up, and gushed a little.

"Christ, you are needy," he hissed. Digging his fingers into my thighs as he dipped his head and sucked on my clit.

Warmth dropped onto my thighs and I knew it wasn't from him. My cheeks blazed anew as I finally managed to unhook my bra and threw the offending garment as far as I could. What started life as a small cry ended as a heady scream when Will nipped my clit between his teeth and sucked at the same time.

That scream echoed around us, filtering down the mountainside as I bucked beneath him. Strong hands pinned me into a place where he refused to let me up until I screamed again, this time with his name on my lips.

"Please," I was back to begging, but I no longer cared about the whys or anything else, needing him to stop torturing me. I spread my legs wider, sending him inside me and a moment later wrapped my thighs around his shoulders, aching for him to be closer. "Will, please–"

Two fingers thrust straight inside me and I came hard at the intrusion as he flicked my clit with the tongue fast and light. His fingers didn't stop pumping either as I rode his hand. Bliss obliterated everything, the view, the ground beneath us, everything but his arms around me holding me to his body. Everything but his name on my lips, my need to call him to me, pull him deeper into me.

"Fuck," he growled, his mouth slamming onto mine, glossy and wet and tasting like me.

I moaned as he pressed his cock between my legs, reaching for him. He knocked my hand away impatiently, leaning back to tear into a crinkly pack and rolled a condom onto his length. I watched him through hazy eyes. My legs spread wide and draped over his hips. Will fisted his hard length in one hand, stroking between my legs with his other.

"Do you need me to stop?" he asked, breathing hard. "Tell me, Cass." His voice strained, but he asked and I knew if I hadn't known already, that would be the moment I loved him right then.

"If you walk away now, I'll stalk you for the rest of your life," I joked faintly, running my fingers along the top of his thigh. "Please, will. I want this really badly. So much. A lot—"

He leaned forward and pushed inside me.

A scream built at the back of my throat but he stole that too, slanting his mouth over mine as he settled his weight over me. I panted hard for a moment into his mouth, torn between moaning and a full emotional and sensory overwhelm.

"Fuck," I whispered, clasping my hands around his shoulders, and holding on. My nails dug into his skin and even though I knew he'd hurt a little before, Will gave me no sign right now. "This is—"

"Am I hurting you?" Will braced one forearm beside me, lifting his chest off mine.

I urged him back down. "Don't you dare go anywhere. I need you right here." I squeezed my nails into his back, just a little, and he lowered his body back so we were chest to chest, sharing every breath.

"Like this?" he murmured, brushing his mouth over mine, his hips flexing slightly.

"Just like that," I whispered as he began to move.

And then I couldn't talk, not at all, and when he kissed me and didn't stop, I didn't try to. Will made love to me under the fall Montana sun, letting me wrap my legs around his thighs, cradling me in his arms as I arched and came around him. He never stopped and he never rushed us. And he never let me rush him, no matter how I dug my nails into his back or my heels into his ass, tilting my hips upward and silently begging for more.

I didn't know how many times I came around him, only that our bodies were covered in a sheen of sweat that pooled between us. His hold on me never wavered, and his kisses never stopped. Finally, the sensations became too much. I flung my head back, breaking the kiss as the next orgasm rent something deep inside me. My scream echoed back off the mountainside at us, and Will's arms tightened around me.

"Fuck honey. That's a beautiful sight." I came down from my Will-induced high to find him staring down at me, absolutely still for the first time. "Can you do that for me one more time?"

I stared up at him, his face dark, then realized how dark it had become around us. Clouds set in behind him and a cool breeze brushed my over-heated face in the lightest kiss.

"Once more," I breathed, unable to promise him anything else just then.

He watched me for a moment longer, leaned down to kiss my swollen lips and caught my knee, lifting it over his shoulder. One hand braced behind my head, the other cupped the back of my neck as he flexed his hips deep, snapping them at the end of his thrust. A yelp tore from me that I didn't think I'd be able to give after the magnitude of my last orgasm, and a groan echoed above me.

"Gonna be rough and fast, okay honey?" Will warned me, his eyes as wild as the sky above us.

I nodded, gripping his biceps tight, unable to close my hands around them.

That was all the permission he needed, driving his hips forward until my cries filled the cliff line, and my throat turned raw. But I couldn't look away from the man above me as I clung to him. His eyes locked onto mine, refusing to look away as he thrust deep inside me, once more and again, touching some part of me so hidden I didn't think I'd ever be able to find it. Some part of me that was made for him.

I screamed again as my body tightened around his, drawing him deeper, vaguely away from Will's shout as came with me, both of us lost and tumbling endlessly, but together.

And then we were holding each other, wrapped around each other's bodies. I let out a sob into his chest as he stroked my hair.

"Christ, it took too long for us to be together."

Will buried his face in my hair. "I'm sorry, Cassie. That should have happened sooner."

I wanted to slap him but I was too tired. "You wore me out," I accused him softly, curling into the space he made for me between his arms, against his heart. "I'm—"

"Perfect," he whispered, kissing me so tenderly that I swore my heart shattered and reformed all at once.

CHAPTER NINE

WILL

Cassie curled next to me in the truck on the way back to the big house. We tried a few more places after a late lunch—a really late lunch. My knees ached and a few more things, though the benefits of our marathon lovemaking session far outweighed the cons in my book. I hoped she felt the same way, and from how she leaned onto my side, my jacket draped over her tiny, curved body, I figured I got that part right, at least. I'd never forget the way she looked, arching beneath me all spread out and flushed as she came again and again.

We tried to find our clothes afterward, but not everything turned up the way it should have. Her bra remained AWOL no matter how hard we searched and her white tee that I loved? It suddenly seemed like a not so great idea because while it showcased her curves—*all* of her curves to me without the bars underneath., I could see the outline of her nipples that I had toyed with for the last hours and I didn't want any other man's eyes on them.

So I was kinda glad when the weather closed in and Cassie accepted my jacket, wrapping her up tight. My hands still wandered, but that body of hers I planned upon worshiping plenty of the days he had left? That was for my view alone. Gage might have different views on the matter with his wife and their relationship, but Cass was my girl, I wanted her to myself.

And with the rodeo boys rolling in from after dusk last night to before dawn this morning in their typical style, I didn't doubt there would be plenty of eyes on Cassie, especially ones who knew her.

My arm around her shoulder tightened. I didn't

doubt she was it for me, or even me for her. But I'd heard the doubt in her voice when I talked about the distance between Jude and Natalie, and that hit something deep in my gut. *Hard.*

"Hey, so after the rodeo, I've got a few more weeks of work here, then I can take you back to school if you like. At Montana U. If you're up for another road trip?" I swallowed back the bile that rose in my throat at the thought of leaving her there. Maybe I could get some work at a ranch nearby, but that would clash with the rodeo circuit's start dates and then I'd be out for a full season. In the last few years, I'd never missed a season. Not that I won much money, but sponsorships and earning a name got me paid just enough to keep going and...

Hell.

I rubbed my knuckles across the back of my neck. Who was I kidding? I had nothing to offer a girl like Cassie who came from money and had dreams of her own.

She stiffened beneath my arm and I knew straight away I'd said the wrong thing. "I didn't want to think about leaving," she mumbled into the collar of my jacket.

I hugged her tight to my side. "Forget I said

anything. I don't want to rush this with us," I reassured her. Or tried to.

Her laugh came out hollow, and no amount of leather between her and me could disguise that. "Well, we took over a month to get it on. How much slower could we actually take it?" The dose of scorn in her voice left my jaw tweaking.

I gripped the steering wheel hard enough for the rubber to squeak. "I mean, we could have left it for a —" I closed my mouth with a snap. No way could I tell her that I'd imagined her dressed in something else white and lacy looking at the outdoor chapel behind Red Hart where Travis and Rachel were married. Another couple who spent time apart because Rachel had her own vet's practice and Travis ran Red Hart. I pulled the truck up and pressed my lips fiercely to Cassie's temple, turning her to face me.

"Listen to me, Cassie. I don't want to take you back to college. Hell, I don't want to take you anywhere at all. I want to stay right here with you. But this isn't my home. It's not my place. I have no idea where that is at all, but—" I frowned when I realized her eyes weren't focused on my face. Cass stared over my shoulder, her gaze slightly vacant. In all the times we'd talked and she'd sassed me—and that was still sexy as all hell—she'd never flat out ignored me. "Cass?" I pressed a knuckle beneath her chin and lifted her face up to mine, peering at her. "Honey, did I scare you?"

Cassie blinked. Her gaze shifted to focus on mine. "Smoke," she whispered.

I stared hard at her, and twisted in my seat, already swearing. I'd been so wrapped up in my thoughts about the girl beside me that I'd been too blind to see what was right in front of me. Fine tendrils of smoke melded with the growing afternoon haze just feet ahead of us. Faint here, but as I peered through the trees, the haze grew.

I grabbed my phone off the dash and shoved it into Cassie's hands, yanking the seatbelt across her chest that I hadn't made her wear as we meandered out way across the ranch on our way back, taking our timer. The damn thing finally *snicked* as I shoved it into place.

"Call," I snapped. "Travis or Jude."

Cassie's fingers flew over the keypad once I opened it for her, and she spoke quietly, no sigh of panic in her voice as we pushed through the haze. Thankfully it thinned out fast as we moved toward the house. I pointed out a few landmarks for her, and she relayed those to Travis, or whoever picked up on the other end.

Finally, I drove into the yard and pulled her into me for a quick, hard kiss. "I'm gonna have to run." I stared down at her regretfully, memorizing the pretty shape of her eyes, wishing it was her bed I'd fall into later tonight, though my lump borrowed mattress would have to do. "I'll try to find you if we don't come in too late, okay?"

She returned my gaze just as fiercely, unflinching. "I'll be here, Will." Soft lips pressed to mine, then she flurried out of my car, leaving my phone in the warm spot where she'd sat tucked in beside me the entire trip back to the big house.

"Damn, that girl's got you spinning, hasn't she?" Gage hung in the door Cassie just vacated.

I glared at the older soldier turned cowboy. "Isn't it your bedtime, old man?" I groused, wishing I had just a few extra minutes with my girl. "I was looking forward to a quiet night with her, maybe—"

"Get laid like you tried last night and fucking failed?" Gage snorted. "Nice try, kid."

I shook my head and said nothing.

His shrewd eyes missed nothing. "Instead, you raised hell after doing just that, huh? We all gotta join your post coital party? Get your ass out here and help, huh?"

He slammed my door shut hard enough to make me wince and pray the damn thing didn't fall off and show the rust underneath that made the price tag affordable for my wallet when I bought it. Thankfully, everything stayed as it should. I climbed out to find Cassie exiting the house I thought she'd just headed into, bearing bundles of blankets and a plastic container of foot. She nudged a second container forward that held a collection of drink bottles. From the sound of its scrapes across the veranda, they were full.

I took the steps two at a time and collected them from her. "Hey, you don't have to be a one woman army, you know." I kissed her because I could and everyone had better be too busty prepping for whatever the hell was coming before I grabbed the water bucked and layered the sandwich container on top. "What are the blankets for? I don't think we're camping out in a wildfire, honey."

She huffed and stalked past me, dropping the bundle that looked heavier than it should be on the back of my truck. Water dripped out of the bottom of the pile. "Some are damp. They're for it if you catch fire or something needs to be damped out that shouldn't be ablaze, okay?" She looked up at me with worried eyes. "Do you remember what I said?"

I scraped her hair back from her face. "That you'll wait up?" The thought of her being there for me when I crawled my smoky, dusty ass back through those doors tonight kindled something different inside me.

"Yeah, that's what I said. I'll be here, Will Kirk. Right here." She pointed to the dirt she stood on.

I hauled her into my chest in a tight hug and kissed the top of her head. "Go inside, Cassie," I murmured to the top of her head. "I reckon it's warmer in there, and you can do something other than watch for us. That's a shit job, am I right?"

She looked up at me and swallowed hard, then turned and ran back up the stairs, almost colliding face first with Travis who headed out of the house at the same time. He looked at me with raised eyebrows. I shrugged as he put on his boots, followed by Rachel who ignored his own orders to stay put with a shake of her head.

Eve and Jude were nowhere in sight. I figured one was already at the site of the fires, doing a little reconnaissance and the other was inside. No brownie points for guessing which was which, and though I knew Jude possessed the patience of several saints rolled into one, waiting wasn't his style.

"Alright, listen up," Travis called from the top of the stairs as both rodeo crew and the ranch hands gathered around the yard. He motioned them closer. "I have no idea what it looks like apart from the fact that we've seen a few fires around and the conditions are right for a wildfire. We want to stop this thing from getting any bigger, because that makes it damn hard to stop, and out here, that's deadly. There aren't that many places out here, and if you're looking for the local fire brigade, turn to the man beside you and say hello."

That little one linter earned the ranch owner a decent laugh, breaking some of the tension in the yard.

"Jude's already out there, so take his direction once you hit the ground. Your other crew chiefs tonight are myself, Gage," Travis paused to locate the man who raised a hand to identify himself, "and Will. Where the hell are you, Will? Damn, you're shrinking by the day," Travis called out. "You'd better stay on a bull better than that or we won't be able to find you at all."

I gave him an easy wave as the rodeo crew behind me had a decent laugh.

One of the older riders, Denver, who I respected, clapped my shoulder. "I mean, he's not wrong about the bull."

My wave turned into a one finger salute over my shoulder and Denver laughed.

Travis gave everyone a hard stare after he organized teams. "Most of you are familiar with the land, so follow Will back to the site. It's dusk and the land changes. Follow the direction of your crew chief tonight, and we should do fine. If there's a problem and you lose contact, grab the numbers from Gage, who has everyone's plus the house. The girls inside will be here in case it gets out of hand and we need to call in extra help. Clear?"

I knew they would have already, but it made the new crew feel a whole lot better about it. I gave one last glance at the house and headed for my truck, praying it would be a quick and easy job, and we'd all be back chatting around the table telling stories before full dark with Cassie in my arms.

CHAPTER TEN

CASS

Waiting sucked.

Waiting in someone else's home when I had no idea when any of Red Hart's impromptu fire crew would be back was worse. I migrated from the kitchen to the veranda and back again before Eve called me over to the sofa in front of the fire once dark fell in full.

"Sit," she instructed me, passing me a full bowl of noodles with vegetables and a boiled egg floating on top. "Eat. You'll feel better."

I poked the egg with my finger and accepted the spoon she passed to me, then the chopsticks. "Ah, I'm not so good with those."

Eve laughed at me outright. "You go to college, right? Aren't college students still broke?"

"Well, yes, and no." I shrugged, uncomfortable as always with the topic of my family. "I get a pretty decent allowance as long as I attend classes. If I don't...no income. No income, no food."

Eve studied me for a moment. "And yet you're not riding the easy street and studying, despite that Will tells me you have a passion for what you do."

"Will should learn not to divulge my secrets." I changed from poking my boiled egg with my finger to poking it with my chopsticks. Maybe I could impale it and manage to catch it that way? The spoon looked twice as dangerous. I doubted Eve would appreciate me slinging my dinner halfway across her sofa.

"He talks when he thinks someone is listening." Eve watched me play with my dinner and sighed. "Hold out your hand." She fixed my chopsticks and my grip so I had pincers going. "Is that better? I have animal ones for kids in the drawer if you need them."

I giggled. "I mean, I could, just for the hell of it but...this seems to work."

I managed to eat my noodles and even conquered the egg after a few false starts, one of which included dunking the smooth object straight into the middle of the bowl. Thankfully that happened just as Jude called, and Eve turned her back as I splashed myself in the face with miso soup.

"...if you say so. When? Alright. I'll tell her." Eve wandered past and I caught a part of her conversation with Jude. I knew I shouldn't but my ears straightened as I finished my soup. "No, it's fine. I said fine. Yes, She'll be fine." Eve's voice dropped an octave as she wandered around the other side of the kitchen and out of sight.

Even I knew better than to argue with Eve when she used the 'F' word after working with her for the past weeks. If *fine* came into play, then the world was about to end.

I carried my bowl to the sink and washed it up, turning to place it in the cupboard and found Eve standing right behind me.

"Fuck," I muttered, and clamped a hand over my

mouth. I'd never sworn in front of her before. "I' m sorry." I frowned. Her face was unusually still. I wondered if we were still in a 'fine' moment. "Are you okay?"

"I'm good."

"Okay." *Good* was a short graduation form *fine*, but only a short step along the chain. I rolled my lips inward. "Is everyone else okay?"

Will.

Oh, fuck. Please let Will be okay. Please, please, please let him be okay.

My mind raced through everything that could possibly go wrong during wildfire hour. A tree branch fell on him, and he was injured. His clothing caught fire and he got burned. He inhaled smoke. That could cause plenty of problems of its own. Wait, he wasn't asthmatic, was he? I ran back through everything I knew about Will Kirk, which, admittedly, was not a whole lot.

He's a generous lover who holds me afterwards when I cry.

He spends hours sitting beside me when I'm busy just to spend time together.

He works hard, and will take me anywhere I want to go, when I want, even when it's got nothing to do with him.

He can't stay on a bull for eight seconds.

I huffed at that last one despite the truth in it. I had seen him ride and seen him tumble.

I'd also seen him get up and climb that railing to an arena full of cheers that turned into chants of his name. Because Will Kirk, with his infectious smile and easy nature, was a crowd pleaser, and everyone loved him.

Including me.

Definitely me.

I squeezed my eyes shut, unwilling to hear whatever Eve had to say, but needing to know all the same. *Waiting really does suck.* "What happened?" I pushed out.

"Austin's been hurt."

I opened my eyes and peered at her. "What?"

Eve frowned. "Austin. The big guy with the red face who tells tall tales? He is your brother, isn't he? Or is he your cousin?"

I shook my head in the face of her confusion. "Yes, he's my brother. I'm sorry. I just thought— What happened?" I covered my screw up with a cough, but Eve was already talking.

It's not Will. It's not Will.

My brain fogged up with internal cheers while Eve told me a story about Austin wandering off into a smoke haze from a fire that wasn't even on Red Hart land, *her* land, and through a fence line that had broken. He promptly fell off the edge of a short cliff that ended—thankfully—with a quick drop straight onto a rock face that left him slightly bloodied and disoriented.

"They're checking him for concussion now, and some of the boys will take him down to our local doctor. Dave is..." She cleared her throat. "Experienced. I'm sure he'll be great. And they can take him to White Cap if he needs further treatment or if he needs anything more."

"Okay," I murmured, squeezing my hands together. "Did you hear anything else? What are they doing? When will they be back? How big is this thing?"

I could have kept going with my questions, but I called it there. The rodeo boys didn't know Red Heart Land. Hell, I didn't know the land, but the ranchers did. The two teams barely knew each other. So much could go wrong and Austin already got hurt. I knew I should be more worried about him but it sounded like he was being taken care of and let's be honest, Austin did stupid shit all our live and managed to survive into his mid twenties so far. I bit my lip, waiting for answers and tried not to bounce on my toes. If Eve didn't get my point, then my cause was beyond lost.

She smiled gently at me. "I'm sure they'll be back soon. Keep your phone on, and Will might call or message before they head back, okay? Oh—" She held up her own phone as it buzzed at her, picking up the call and talking and she walked, heaving up the stairs away from me.

"Guess it's just me, then." I went outside to sit on the veranda again, staring into the trees across the broad paddock where I thought we had been this afternoon and where we had seen the smoke, but I had no idea really where that was. The longer I stared, the sleepier I became.

With no flickering lights or trail of smoke as a point of reference, there was nothing to look at. I headed back inside, hoping that Eve would be about, but I could hear her faint murmurs from upstairs. The formidable Archer, I assumed, was the other half of the phone call.

Sighing, I checked my phone and sent off a quick message.

CASSIE: *Let me know if you're alright.*

CASSIE: *Hoping the only injury is my wayward sibling and that everyone else is okay.*

I bit my lips and managed not to send anything

else, but no three dots came back at me. Will was probably so busy with everyone that he wouldn't have a chance to check his phone. Mine, however, blinked at me with a low battery symbol turned red and empty.

Shuffling over to the sofa, I put mine on charge, and rested my head back. My eyes drifted shut as I flapped about a crocheted rug I'd spotted on the arm of the chair previously. That was blessedly in range, and so I pulled it over myself, curling into a Cassie sized ball in the corner.

Then my eyes drifted shut and I dreamed of smoke filled caves and warm hugs beneath too hot clothes. Finally, I kicked out a foot that connected with something solid.

"Ow, girl. That hurt," my dream grumped at me.

"You what?" I sat up, or tried to, but my dream also had arms as well as a solid form, and pulled me back to his chest as I blinked myself awake, still on the sofa beside the fire.

I tried to twist about, but arms looped around me securely.

"You know, I was perfectly comfortable with you right where you were, Cassie." Will's voice registered through my sleep filled haze.

Those arms slid along my ribs and lifted me

against his body, resettling me over his chest. The familiar rhythm of his heart thumped beneath my cheek. I twisted m y fingers in the soft material of his shirt and let it plop back onto his chest. Even in the dim moonlight I could make out the RHR antlered logo in contrast against the pale material.

"You borrowed this," I murmured, yawning. "That seemed like cheating. I burrowed into his chest. "Wait, why aren't we in my bed?"

"Because the only way Travis would let me stay with you was if I slept on the sofa, with you, and you didn't scream bloody murder the moment I touched you."

"Oh. Didn't I?" I asked, interested.

"No, you snored instead. Trav was grossly disappointed," Will murmured, stroking my hair back from my face with gentle fingers. "It was fairly cute though."

"I'm so glad to entertain you. What time did you get back?" I stifled another yawn against his chest. "What time is it now?"

"Three in the morning now and midnight or just after when we came in. The fire wasn't on Red Hart land and it was pretty small. Apparently someone dumped a heap of rubbish on a neighboring property. Some trespassers, who knows. There was a lot of glass, and it looks like maybe some of it caught alight. It's a good thing that while it was a warm day, it wasn't stupidly hot and there was no wind to make it worse."

I sank against him. "That's good," I sniffed. "You don't smell like bacon."

He laughed beneath me. "Is that what you think I'm supposed to smell like after attending a wildfire, honey?"

I shrugged. "I don't know. But you smell good, and you aren't supposed to smell like soap. I'm pretty sure of that."

He laughed. "Yeah, well Travis didn't want me on his soda smelling like barbecue, that's for damn sure. Now get some sleep before we have to get up in a few hours and set up the rodeo for tomorrow night."

"Oh. I forgot. That came up soon."

"It did."

"Font' fall off your bull, okay? I need some street cred around here. Dust cred? Dirt cred." I considered my options.

"Please stop." Will pressed his lips to the top of my head, adjusting my blanket. His arms tightened around me. "Goodnight, Cassie."

"Night, Will." I yawned again, nestling into him, already half drifting off. "Love you."

His hands stilled on my back before they resumed stroking me gently, lulling me into sleep. "I love you too, Cass. Go to sleep."

But I was already gone.

.

CHAPTER ELEVEN

WILL

I finally woke up with Cassie on my chest, and she felt so damn good I never wanted to move. But even though the boys and a handful of the Red Hart women crawled into their beds just after midnight, I knew the core crew would be up shortly and...I needed time with my girl before the house got busy.

And hell, she threw me like a raging rodeo bull

telling me she loved me the night before, but I'd live that ride over and over if it meant feeling her snuggle into me when she did. I doubted she even remembered. The words just seemed to flow out of her. After the mess of everything last night after our perfect day together at the ridge yesterday, I knew I'd have that moment on replay in my mind forever.

Even so, I lay there when I should have been moving, stroking her hair, enjoying the way her languid body sort of flowed into mine. Our legs tangled beneath the blankets I tossed over us when I came in the night before after showering, trying to scrub the smoke out of my hair and off my skin with scalding water that I managed to claim for the first time this season—and on the right day, for once.

Cassie's head rested over my chest, her cheek pressed above my heart. Every breath tightened my ribcage until I thought it might burst. I'd had plenty of rodeo flings and a girlfriend or two back in high school but never anything serious. Hell, I hadn't been in one place long enough to have anything serious, and the sorts of girls I hooked up with were the one night only type events. Good time girls who usually sought me out after a hard ride, or in the bar afterward, or someone Denver threw in my path while I was licking my wounds.

Burt Cassie... She was just sort of there that night. We fell into each other and never let go.

"And I never will," I murmured, trailing my fingers along her spine, and rested my hand across her back.

She appeared so tiny there that my fingers splayed out and took up most of the space. Hell, two of my hands could probably crush her. She looked so fragile there, curled on my chest, but I knew she was strong beyond belief, even if her brother and family, from what I gathered, didn't share the same opinion.

"Morning," Cassie murmured, rubbing her nose on my shirt. "You still don't smell like smoke. It's disconcerting." She blinked up at me twice and wiggled her perfect ass.

"It's okay. You smell pretty enough for both of us," I told her, unable to smile as my heart lodged somewhere in the realm of my throat and refused to budge. I rubbed a thumb along her spine until I reached her nape and pulled her up my body, drawing a gasp from her as I settled her close enough to kiss. "Everyone's gonna be up soon, honey. Can you be quiet for me while I steal a few more moments with you?"

Her eyes shone as she woke from her doze in full

a second before I cupped her nape and pulled her mouth down to mine.

Soft lips parted on a sigh heady enough to harden me on demand. I palmed her ass with my other hand, pushing her down onto me, rocking us gently together until she moaned into my mouth.

"Shh," I cautioned her softly. "Easy, honey." I stroked her hair, tangling my fingers through her blonde waved and held her in place as I kissed her back, pushing her lips wide and explored her mouth.

Her breath stuttered as she held in the noises I loved yesterday from her. My cock swelled knowing she struggled for me, the tip of her tongue gliding along the length of mine in a show of sweet submission. I swallowed hard when she rubbed her body against mine, and dropped my hand from her hair to slide beneath her hoodie—*my* hoodie that she'd borrowed at some point—and cupped her breast, tugging the nipple free of her bra.

I rolled the tight bud between my fingers in a slow rhythm I knew she liked, pressing her ass down against mine in the same way without letting her up for air. She struggled for a moment, the softest huffs against my lips the prettiest sounds.

A low growl left my throat in warning, and she settled against me, letting me play. Christ, she felt too damn good against me. There were too many clothes in the way, and all I wanted was to strip her bare and fuck her raw beneath me. But that would have to wait for another time without so many people likely to be present shortly. My kisses grew harsher, and I knew I bruised her lips by the way she softened hers, but Cassie never pulled away or complained, pressing her breast into my palm, rocking her hips into the rhythm I set.

I sent a mental promise that I'd reward her when we found time away from everyone else again for giving me this moment together as soon as we could. The rodeo would be hellishly busy and I knew from past experience that we'd barely find time together. This was my chance to savor as many moments with Cassie as I could. What started as a sweet, pre-dawn morning make out session quickly devolved into something far more carnal.

Cassie moaned softly into my mouth as I slid my fingers along the seam of her jeans over her hot little slit. She hadn't gotten changed the night before, and fell asleep in her clothes waiting for me. I'd picked her up when Travis let me into the big house, sliding in beneath her and settling her over my body until we woke together again after our stunted conversation the night before that would be seared into my memory forever. That memory kept me going now as I traced the shape of her through her jeans. The shape of her was all too easy to feel and I wondered if she had panties on or not beneath her clothes.

The thought left me rock hard. I broke our kiss with a soft groan I couldn't suppress, pinching her nipple hard as I rubbed her denim seam. Cassie moaned into my shirt, the sound muffled, thankfully as she burrowed into the blankets. Her hips worked frantically against mine and I closed my eyes in fucking pure bliss at the feel of her using my body to get herself off.

This wasn't how I expected this morning to go, if I expected anything at all, but fuck was I here for it.

I milked her nipple with my fingertips, swirling and tugging until her body shuddered. Her thighs tensed and heat flushed my fingers over her jeans. I pressed those to her body as she rode the waves of her orgasm out, leaving me hard and aching, but fucking pleased that she'd come for me.

"So beautiful," I murmured, gliding her back up my body from where she had pooled into the middle of my chest, to meld our mouths together in a long, slow kiss.

And then we lay there together until the sun broke across the far ridge line, painting Red Hart's fields in a perfect display of crisp golden light without a flicker of smoke in sight.

If the house filled with people too fast for me to detangle from Cassie an hour after I woke her with kisses that turned too much, too fast for both of us, then the yard and the field beyond became something chaotic within minutes after the full rodeo crew descended in all their glory the moment we all caffeinated after Eve pumped us full of food and let us roam free.

For the first time in years I wasn't part of setting up the arena. Instead, I rounded up the herd, moving them into fields away from the crowd where they wouldn't get hurt or spooked by the noise of us all in the next hours.. The stink of the bulls freaked the poor critters out so damn bad that I had leaping fawns, some who were just losing their spots and separating from their mothers, bounding about everywhere. Worse, I got to be in charge of Austin who had returned from his trip for a short rock with a short stop when he crashed back first into a granite shelf the night before, wandering about lots in the smoke because he couldn't follow directions.

Or refused to.

Hell didn't come close to covering it.

"Catch him. That one," I called to Luke, who swept his arms wide and used the fence line like a pro to herd the bouncing fawn into the next paddock. He grabbed the gate and ran it in, closing the deer in, catching another on the way through and sent me a thumbs up.

"Fucking brilliant. That leaves us..." I turned to count heads in the large paddock we were in. We'd moved nearly ninety of the suckers, and I was shattered. I'd better draw a bull called *Driving Miss Daisy* or else I had no chance tonight of making points on anything.

At least I knew I'd score with a pretty girl afterwards. The thought of holding Cassie in my arms held me in place for a moment, just long enough to miscount one of the damn fawns who slithered under my knees and knocked me on my ass.

"Good practice for tonight," Austin groused at me from his place at another gate where he did what I'd expected when I got lumped with him—fucking nothing.

He'd been cleared for all signs of concussion. No injuries, breaks or bruises, except maybe to his ego. But the moment Denver heard about it, he refused to have him on the rodeo set up. And so, he was officially my responsibility. The man who hated me more than anyone in the world, and now I was dating his sister.

Fucking brilliant.

"Be better if you helped," I snapped back, "than stand there and direct."

"Someone has to do it," Austin drawled.

And shut up.

I seethed, squeezing the fence with my gloved hand and wished it was his neck. My eyes shut for a second and a shadow fell over me. Hell, maybe he had actually moved his ass like I demanded. I waited for the punch to the face that habitually followed but when I opened my eyes, Noah and Luke stood in front of me, Luke's hand extended.

"We got you, boss." Noah winked. "Apparently Austin's bull tonight is a bit of a spinner."

I blinked at them and grinned. "Now, boys. We can't go fixin' the draw. That's not fair to a big guy like him."

They both laughed at me, but I meant it. If either of us won or lost, I wanted it to be a fair round. Actually, I was surprised that Denver was letting Austin ride at all. Usually, he refused to let injured—even semi injured—riders on a bull, but he must have bullied the doc into letting him walk away with a clean bill of health. I needed to have a word with Denver about that draw, though.

I cleared my throat, taking Luke's hand and let the other ranch hand pull me out of the dirt. No doubt I'd be back in it later tonight just like Austin crowed about, but my ego wasn't as big as the rich boy's, and falling didn't hurt half as much for me when I'd spent my rodeo career right there in the dust where I started.

"Alright." I swiped grit off my ass and tightened my gloves, counting heads. Deer, not ranch hands or ring ins. "We've got six of these pretty little things to go. And I bet Miss Eve has a handful of beers for the men who bring them in, am I right?"

Noah and Luke cheered, while Austin sent me an *are you fucking insane* glance, but he didn't get ranch culture. He'd never been rationed to one-beer-a-day for a season, and an extra beer on rodeo night after catching runaway fawns and does mean everything to the boys who busted their asses for me.

Plus, those little suckers we chased were fast fuckers. They'd earn every damn sip. But this time,

I'd make sure that Austin grew red in the face right alongside us. *Direct my boys, my ass.* I fixed him a hard look as I handed out directions, setting the boys to herd in the last few fawns. The does followed in, keen to still be with their offspring, and naturally, the last to come in was Snowball.

The pale little fawn who was fast maturing into a juvenile bounced about, completely oblivious to the chaotic noise factor about him in his muted world.

"That one's yours, Austin!" I bellowed, grabbing the gate and pulled it wide.

A little too wide as Austin lumbered behind the randy deer spawn. Snowball shot between us and tangled around my ankles. I clung to the gate, determined not to eat dirt again before tonight's main event.

"Fuck's sake, Will, can't you do anything right?" Austin cursed.

I smirked. "All you gotta do is be fast, big fella." I leaned down and scooped Snowball into my arms. Hooves flailed about until he saw it was me. Then he quietened, and offered me a tentative lick on my dust face with his long, pink tongue. We both wrinkled our noses at the smelly, gritty after effect.

"Not the action I was hoping to get today, lil' guy," I told him affectionately, plopping him down in his new field next to a doe I thought was his mother.

He took one look at her, glanced back at me and skittered off.

"Guess you got that one wrong, boss," Luke nudged me quietly as Austin muttered to himself, bullying dust bunnies in a cloud behind us.

"Can't win 'em all," I mused, leaning back against the gate.

Snowball bounded about on the other side, leaping from doe to doe while I splashed water in my face to remove the scent of stinky fawn breath and ruminated on how a red, sweaty face really did improve Austin's looks after all.

CHAPTER TWELVE

Cassie

Red Hart's yard was packed with people. I didn't recognize half of them but it seemed like Eve and the rest of the RHR regulars knew *everyone*. I wandered at Eve's side, my vision blitzed out by the stadium sized lights that illuminated the entire ranch from mountain to mountain. For the first time after dark I could see everything. The fields stretched out either side of the ranch, treed foothills disappearing into the sides of the mountains that left the big house to one side of the gully.

A rodeo arena had been set up in the field directly opposite the house just outside the yard where everyone else parked and milled about. I was glad we had a place to stay, because I'd hate to have to move my car any time soon. Vehicles were parked end to end in neat rows where Jude and a handful of ranch hands in high vis neon vests directed traffic as locals piled in from neighboring farms.

Considering how remote Red Hart appeared when I first pulled into the property with Will, it didn't seem as though there were that many farms about. But the event had boosted the local population into action. Headlights still lined the long drive as I peered about Eve's shoulder into the distance where I thought the road was further along the few rambling hillocks to the big branded sign bearing all her work.

"They just keep coming," I muttered in something akin to awe, wrapping my arms around myself.

Eve had insisted I borrow a black top of hers, a one-shouldered stretchy affair shot with silver thread that left my back bare beneath my hair if I took my jacket off—also borrowed—and black. I tried to sneak

Will's hoodie into tonight's wardrobe, but Eve wasn't having any of it, and stole it away, promising I could have it back at the end of the night. At least I got to wear my own jeans and boots. My hair hung past my shoulders, wild and free because Eve also styled that. By the time she was done I felt less like me and more like a toy doll, Red Hart style. Right up until she whispered, 'he'll love it," in my ear, and walked away.

And when I looked at just-mussed-hair me with the smokey eyes in the mirror, wearing black and silver, with a pair of dangly earrings and peeking a little bare skin as I walked, I had to agree.

Will might actually go a little nuts after the way he touched me today. I swallowed at the memory of our morning make out session on the sofa before everyone else got up that grew hot and heavy pretty fast. My jeans still smelled faintly like him, and I squeezed my thighs together at the memory of how he'd made me come for him again just with a few touches. I swore that man knew my body far too well. I missed him so much, and I hadn't seen him since breakfast when Eve placed two thermoses of coffee in front of my face and a chopping board to one side.

Five loaves of bread followed and I was a sand-wich machine from there on in, buttering and stacking bacon and eggs like a pro within seconds. By the time I locked up, Will and half the kitchen was empty, and people milled about outside, getting their jobs for the day before the rodeo started in full. I vaguely recalled his kiss on my cheek before he left, and that mark stayed with me through the day.

I stuck my hands into the jacket cropped at my waist and scanned the crowd for Will's familiar form but I couldn't spot him. Gage passed us as Eve diverted to talk to someone else she knew, and a fresh cup of hot coffee in a takeaway cup marked *Beanie's* was thrust into my hand by a woman with a beaming smile who talked over the top of everyone else.

"Thanks!" I yelled over the crowd. "Is this for Eve?"

"It's yours!" she yelled back, pointing to thick black lettering in a hand I recognized across the top.

For Cassie. Love, Will.

Oh, fuck. That wasn't a dream after all.

My world stopped while the chaos of the Reed Hart rodeo fluctuated around me in a swirl of color and lights. I stared at those words for heartbeats that took too long, my blood sluggish as they permeated my brain.

He said it back.

I said it first.

Fuck, fuck, fuck.

I was half asleep when he came in. Actually, scratch that. I'd been fully asleep and I hadn't meant to say that to him, or anything at all. It'd just kinda of slipped on out because I'd been thinking about it for a while now and...

It was true.

I squeezed my eyes shut, probably marrying all of Eve's beautiful handiwork, and sucked in a handful of breaths that refused to sink into my lungs or go further than my throat. Something was in the road. My brain, maybe. Or my heart.

Or my soul.

Because that was the sort of limit that Will Kirk hit on me. Soul deep. And I knew it. He was that deeply etched in me and walking away from him at the end of this would hurt like hell. I didn't just love him.

I loved him. With everything I had.

Breaking out of my haze, I opened my eyes and snagged Gage's sleeve as the older ranch hand strode past. Lost in my head I felt like everything had taken minutes when barely a breath had passed.

"Have you seen Will?" I yelled, my voice straining in an attempt to get above the cacophony ringing between my ears.

Gage met my eyes and raised his gaze over my head as hands settled on my waist.

"Here."

I nearly spilled my coffee as I spun in a circle to face Will. His grin sharpened into something wicked, his eyes sweeping over me to settle back on my face.

"Damnit, Will," I muttered, biting my lip. Butterflies rioted around my ribcage. Inside or out, I couldn't tell. "Was this you?" I waved the coffee in his face.

He squeezed my sides tight. "Better not be anyone else with my name telling you they love you," he murmured, low enough for the words to reverberate along my spine, pulling me close enough for me to hear him over the crowd. "I like this look on you."

"Just like?" I sassed him, looking up through my lashes. I mean, a girl didn't go to college without a few tricks.

"I like." His thumbs brushed over the skin on my belly where my top had ridden up in a sensual gesture that reminded me of...other things. "Are you ready for tonight? I think we're about to start."

Energy buzzed off him that I hadn't seen before. Mind, I met Will after he fell off the last bull he rode so, I hadn't seen this part of him at all before and it was...

Electrifying.

I drew back to study him in full. A black shirt with long sleeves decorated at the collar and cuffs with white and silver piping highlighted his full chest and narrow waist where the shirt tucked into a fresh pair of jeans. Aqua and black fringed chaps hung from his hips over a fresh pair of jeans and his dress boots.

A belt buckle I hadn't seen before rested at his waist. I reached out and ran my thumb across the bull standing still with a rider on its back before a cross.

"What's this?" I looked up as his smile disappeared.

"My grandfather used to ride. He was damn good, too. Won a few things. Thought he might wanna see this ride tonight." A muscle in his jaw ticked beneath the bright lights. For a moment I thought he might say more, but he didn't.

Will looped his hand around mine, drawing me through the crowd. I clung to my coffee, grateful for the path he carved. Eve spotted us as we passed, giving a little wave. I raised my coffee in salute, managed to take a sip, and kept walking.

We wove our way through the crowd until we reached a spot near the edge of the arena, away from the stands.

"I thought we were heading for the." I pointed to the staggered rows of metal seating the RHR/rodeo boys had erected during the day.

Will laughed, winding an arm around me as he tucked me into his side. "Hell, no. If I'm gonna eat dust tonight, I wanna see your pretty face close up when I do it." He leaned down and kissed me.

I swore the entire arena—crowd, dust, chatter and all—disappeared the moment his lips touched mine. Will's hand cupped the back of my head and my hands grew lighter as he held me close, parting my lips with his and delving deep until I sighed and reached into his embrace.

"Fuck, that's worthy of falling hard and fast," he murmured against my mouth, handing me my coffee back.

"I...what?" I asked, dazed as his hands dropped to my waist again, squeezing gently.

"Think your boy has it bad for you." A deep voice spoke over my shoulder and a large hand jolted Will sideways, though he never let me go, tucking me into his chest and wrapping his arms around me. "Will. Hi, Cassie."

"Denver?" I peered over my shoulder and smiled. "It feels like it's been ages. Where did you park?"

The tall rodeo organizer scratched his chin. "Somewhere I'll never find my trailer, that's for sure. Or get out for the next week." He shrugged like that didn't matter.

Maybe to him, it didn't. The rodeo boys worked on their own timetable apart from during the season. Then it was ride, pack up and move to the next location, set up, ride and do it all over again.

Will wrapped an arm around my waist. "Good thing everyone's staying here for a few days." He pointed out everyone I knew from traveling with Austin. "Flint's riding shortly. I think he's up first. Sammy Littlefield and Jesse Reeves are about as well. Over...there." He pointed at the shute where several sets of shoulders were.

"And Heath's playing rodeo clown, as usual." Denver braced his forearms on the railing beside me, though I felt dwarfed next to him.

He was the only person I'd seen who might actually rival Travis's six foot five height. Speaking of...

"Where's Travis?" I looked around, but couldn't spot the tall ranch owner and in a crowd that shouldn't be possible.

"He's an emcee tonight." Eve slipped into the spot Denver vacated, tipping his hat and murmuring his excuses. "Up there."

I squinted at the spot she pointed to, but all I saw was a dark silhouette on the wrong side of the light from where I stood. "I'll have to trust you. Is Jude riding?" I asked curiously, looking back at Will, who shrugged.

"Hell, no. I'm keeping my feet on Red Hart dirt. Will's the one who likes to get air time around here."

Jude stood behind us when I swiveled about, peeking around Will's bulk. The foreman gave me a quick wink, but maintained his customary unsmiling facade. I'd learned that was his usual exterior, and smiles were rare from him, but that didn't mean he was grumpy.

"Speaking of," Will dipped his head and kissed the slope of my neck, leaving tiny shocks tearing across my skin. "I have to go."

"What, now?" *Already? But I just found you,* I wanted to protest. Instead, I bit my lip and nodded. "Be safe?" I offered.

Will laughed. "That's a first. Usually it's, 'try to stay on the bull, Will,' or some other variation."

I wrinkled my nose. "I'll take you not getting hurt again over making points, big guy. And come back to me?" an ache of desperation rose in my chest, and that last came out so soft that I barely heard my own words. I was pretty sure that he wasn't above the crowd.

"Yeah?" His chin brushed my cheek, grazing my skin with stubble, lifting my face to his. I had time for part of a breath before his mouth was on mine in an all consuming kiss before his hands left me and the contact was broken. When he stepped away from me, the satisfaction in his eyes left me on a slow burn inside. "I'll find you after, okay? Stay with Eve."

"I've got her," Eve said after a moment, when I couldn't answer for myself.

I nodded instead, wiggling my fingers. My arms wrapped about my waist as I watched Will walk away, and suddenly I'd never felt so alone in a crowd of people. Travis began to talk, introducing the riders before their first event, but I didn't hear more than a few muted words.

The girls converged on me. We huddled by the railing off to one side of the tiered seating as the boys all lined up. I spotted a few of the newer ranch hands in there, alongside Will, who stood close to the centre, alongside Denver, decked out all in black top to toe. A huge cheer erupted from the crowd in front of Red Hart's big house as someone played Slade's

Cum On Feel The Noize while the boys walked off stage.

Travis rattled on, thanking the locals for coming and the businesses who had donated their time and effort. I turned out again, watching Will leave the center of the arena.

"Does anyone know what order they come in?" I asked the air in general, not really expecting an answer.

A piece of paper in Eve's handwriting was presented to me by two thick, calloused fingers.

"Here's one someone else prepared for you earlier." I could hear the smirk in his voice, even if I knew it wouldn't be visible on his face.

"Thank you." I took the list, tracing my finger to the bottom of the row to find Will's name.

Last.

"Wow." I had to wait all night just to see him ride.

"It'll be okay. Here." Natalie pushed a premixed can into my hands. "Everything is better with vodka."

I grinned, cracking it open. "I mean, I can't argue with that." Something sweet clashed with something else citrusy that argued with my taste buds the whole way down. I grimaced at my enthusiasm from a moment before but relished the light burn. Eve had been right; I was a college student after all. We had moonshine in the dorms that I swore was single handedly responsible for the bald patch on one leg that never required shaving. "It's good," I managed, trying not to gag on the sweetness overwhelm.

Natalie watched me with a shrewd eye. "Or maybe the girl just wants her vodka straight."

"Sure." I gave her a thumbs up and she nodded decisively, disappearing back into the crowd.

Eve shook her head. "Drinking with Nat is dangerous," she laughed softly. "I should know."

"I sense a story there." I hugged her shoulder, passing over the can of premix. "Do you want this? I don't think I can stomach it."

Eve made a face. "Hell, no. I'm a whiskey girl. Besides, I kinda can't..." She pressed a hand to her stomach where I'd seen her wince in the kitchen once before.

I stared at her hand for a moment before the hint dropped and my eyebrows hiked. "Is that? Are you– I—" I glanced back at Jude who watched me with his standard stoic expression, giving away absolutely nothing at all. "You knew," I accused him, giving her a hug.

"Yep." He watched the first rider come out as the ground rumbled and music played.

I knew it wasn't Will, so I ignored everything. "This is your Texas man?" I asked Eve. "Does he know?" Suddenly, all the midnight calls and early morning texts made a whole lot more sense.

She shook her head. "No. I haven't told him yet." The crowd *oohed* around us just before the buzzer rang.

"And that's Sammy Littlefield not quite making the full eight seconds on his ride. No points scored. Next up is a rider from Red Hart's own, Reggie Carson. He hails from the north and speaks like he's from the south..." Travis continued on with Reggie's biography as I stared at Eve.

"You haven't told him," I repeated, frowning. "Why not?" A little voice inside my head told me that it wasn't my business, but right now after all the hours I spent with Eve, and seeing her here, all the worry she'd had on her face, all the worry we all had for her over the past weeks, I figured that maybe I kinda earned the right.

Maybe. Maybe not. She could tell me to go to hell right now and I'd shut up and watch the boys ride.

Eve's face tightened. "I'm scared," she whispered.

I thought she whispered. I read her lips, and my stomach rolled over on itself. Behind me, Reggie made it out of the Shute before he ate dirt.

"Scared of your man?" I couldn't stop asking questions. "Has he hurt you?"

Will said they had a history I didn't know about. Usually, I let people tell me things and never pried. I figured trust worked that way. But this time, it seemed serious enough to ask. To make sure the woman who had kinda mentored me for the last weeks and opened her home to me was safe.

Eve smiled and it was genuine. "It's okay, Cassie. He won't ever do that. It's just—I've lost a pregnancy before. Months ago. Both were unplanned. Both his," she whispered. "What scares me is the future. How much time is between now and when he's here, and who I'll be when he arrives."

I gripped her hands tight. "If that man loves you like you love him, then nothing will stop him, Eve. And no matter what happens, he will love you for who you are. No matter what," I repeated, squeezing her hands.

She nodded, her face drawn, but she did squeeze back. Behind us, Jude made a noise of approval.

I hadn't known that I wanted or needed his support until that moment, but it felt good to know he had m=our backs.

Natalie squeezed between us, holding out glass bottles with black labels. "I couldn't find vodka," she apologized, "so you get tequila doubles instead. Cheers!" She lifted hers to her lips and took a healthy slug.

Eve and I exchanged glances across the tiny woman's head.

"Told you. Dangerous," Eve mouthed to me.

I shook my head, bemused, and took a sip. My tastebuds sang, and I knew just how much sugar was in that drink to make it palatable enough to hide the alcohol content. Dangerous indeed. I'd had to watch it or I'd be on my ass before Will finished his ride.

Eight bulls and two tequilas later, my skin was either too warm or too numb as I watched the next rider out of shute to Billy Idol's *Rebel Yell*. We sang along until my throat went raw, cheering away. Then Denver was up. His bull burst from the shute, already in midair before the metal gate was all the way clear.

A gasp rang out around the arena, and I started counting automatically in my head. *Three. Four. five.* His hand waved above his head, not touching anything, and I knew he'd make the bell. *Six*. Denver sat tall, moving with his bull, a sweet little thing called Cloudburst. *Seven. Eight.*

The buzzer rang out as Denver made his eight seconds, and slid off his bucking bull like it was the easiest thing in the world. He took a few quick steps and walked across the arena to the fence nearest the crowd, hoisting himself up as he high fived the rodeo clown.

I watched Heath, the resident Aussie on circuit, in his colorful garb and shorts that marked him as a non-rider, round the bull up. His arms were spread wide as he herded the still bucking and kicking animal, despite that his rider had long departed, back to the other side of the arena where the bulls existed.

"Will's up next," Jude gave my shoulder a quick squeeze and withdrew his hand, leaning in to murmur something to Natalie.

A second later her vodka disappeared, and she snuggled into his chest, giggling as she faded into the darkness behind the stands. A pang of loneliness struck my chest, then Travis was introducing Will from his place above everything.

I stared at the shute, trying to make out Will's black shirt and aqua chaps, but the bright light that should have made everything so visible did the opposite, obscuring everything instead.

Hells Bells by AC/DC played loud and clear as Will's shute pulled up. His bull didn't burst out like Denver's ride had. It kind of stood there, like its batteries had worn out. I risked a glance at the paper that the judge had drawn up for me, searching for the bull's name.

Lazybones.

I huffed a laugh, looking back up at Will where he made a show of kicking the bull with his heels and humping up and down to make it go. The crowd laughed, and I grimaced on his behalf but as always, will take the mishap in his metaphorical stride.

"Okay, we're going to try that one again." Travis shifted in his spot as the shute went back down, considering the bull hadn't moved in the first place. "Does anyone think we should give our last rider of the night another go?"

The crowd roared as Travis revved them into a frenzy, and music slammed my eardrums. Someone on the fence will give a thumbs up.

"Aright. Someone gave our resident dust bather a quarter and we've got some action going. Let's give Will Kirk and Lazybones another round of applause because we say they're ready to ride!" Music blitzed the field as the shute opened and lazybones and Will shot out of the opening in a picture perfect entry to the arena.

Dust flew from beneath the bull's hooves, Will's aqua fringed chaps visible from every angle. His back was straight, one hand perfectly in the air. I half wished I'd brought Eve's camera with me for this moment, then remembered to count.

One. Will's bull twisted and turned in spectacular style. If he stayed on, he'd score as well as Denver for this ride.

Two. His seat shifted with Lazybones who tore about the arena, as determined to dislodge his rider as Will was to stay aboard his bull.

A leap, a buck. For a moment the pair hung together in a perfect suspension of dust and sweat, arms and legs extended in a picture perfect finish.

Three.

Will hit the ground before his bull and tasted Red Hart dirt.

CHAPTER THIRTEEN

WILL

Chatter in the big house had been muted all day. Apart from the only Christmas I'd spent at Red Hart, I'd never not worked a day on this land whenever I stayed here. Not even on the day we buried Travis's father. It just seemed the right thing to do. But today, with the rodeo boys still around, and everyone either exhausted, hungover, or both, Jude and Travis called it and we took the day off.

I was happy with that choice as it left me with my arms wrapped around Cassie for the better part of the day. But as much as I loved socializing with friends who I hadn't seen for the last month and that I could relive last night's false start a million times over just for the fun of it, by the time dinner rocked around, I was as tired of seeing other people as my girl was.

I grabbed a hamper out of the pantry, thanked Jude for letting me take off, and grabbed Casie's hand.

"Get your jacket. Some shoes. Anything else you need for the night and meet me out the front," I murmured into her ear, tucking her hair back from her face tenderly.

She twisted to look up at me with tired eyes. "Huh? I think I'm on servery tonight."

I shook my head. "Cleared you already. As soon as you can, okay?" I kissed her temple and headed for the door.

She let out a soft sound behind me, caught somewhere between amusement and exasperation. Some chatter followed her footsteps. Her hand slipped into mine as I pulled my jacket on and helped her into hers.

"Where are we going? You can't possibly get your truck down the drive in that mess." She pointed to the cars and trailers, some occupied, that lined the yard in a gridlock pattern.

I shook my head, grinning, though she probably missed it. "Nope. We're going that way." I pointed toward the trees, and jammed a pair of blankets into the handle of the hamper, along with a rug I tossed over my shoulder, bundled into a sling. "You ready?"

"For what?" Her brow furrowed. "I have no idea what we're doing, Will."

"I owe you a real date. Not the one we had that got interrupted last time." Our perfect day. "Or the morning that we had to give up because we had people around us." There were so many times that I wanted to do things with Cassie in the last weeks, times when I needed him to myself that just hadn't happened. Suddenly, that week driving across the country together seemed wasted. I wished I'd taken more time with her but we weren't new to each other then and the trust we had now hadn't been established between us yet when we first met and decided to go on this whirlwind trip together for the hell of it.

And now here we were.

"You gonna walk into the forest with me, honey?" I held out my hand and prayed she'd take it.

She flicked her hair back and sent me a challenging gaze. "That depends. Are you going to feed me and hold me and show me something amazing?"

I leaned down and caught her mouth with mine in a slow kiss that left us both breathless. "And love you. Deal?"

"Deal," she whispered back.

Then her hand folded into mine, so small and fragile yet tough and perfect, and she walked beside me the whole way into the forest the hour before darkness closed in.

I'd found the perfect spot by accident a week earlier when I was rounding up a doe and her fawn who wandered off along the creek line. Here, just beyond where the river diverted into a small stream, a clearing formed a small divot in the ground. It probably got a little colder overnight, hence the blankets, but we were protected from winds and the waterfall's cool spray just around the bend by a granite outcrop.

Plus, if Cassie didn't like it, I had two other spots nearby kicked out, but we'd be walking there in the dark.

"Is this okay," I asked softly, letting her walk through the pine needle bed scattered beneath her feet as she turned in circles, looking up the tall pines. The small stream gurgled softly beside us, just out of sight. "I figured we could set up here for the night, head back tomorrow sometime, midmorning."

"Don't you have to work?" Cassie finished her circuit of the location and turned back to me. "Won't Jude be pissy at you?"

I huffed a laugh. "I got permission, honey. We're not breaking any rules. Double permission, actually. Travis knows exactly what we're doing and where we are for the night. He's pretty protective of you, actually."

Twice as protective as he'd been of any other girl I'd seen on RHR land other than his sister. Not that it was a bad thing at all. I just figured it would make things tougher when we left.

"Oh. That's really sweet." Cassie worried her bottom lip between her teeth. "Does Eve—"

"Yes. She knows. Do you want me to take you

back? I can if this is too much." I hadn't thought about her being freaked out about staying overnight in the forest. "I've slept out here plenty of nights, Cass. But if it scares you, I'll take you home. Just tell me." I slid my hands around her waist, stepping into her space. "Tell me," I whispered when she stared up at me, her mouth moving but nothing came out.

"I just want you," she breathed.

My mouth crashed into hers, my kisses harsh and desperate. Every inch of pent up energy burst from me and collided with her as I pulled Cassie flush against my body. A soft sound that might have been a sob or a sigh echoed from her lips to mine. I held her tight and kissed her fiercely, pulling back only to check in.

"Tell me again," I asked softly, cradling her face in my hands. "I promise I'll stop any time. But I need you to tell me if there's anything you don't want about tonight."

"Everything I want everything from you." Cass rose onto her toes, finding my mouth as she slid her tongue between my lips.

My cock hardened instantly. I growled softly, kicking the hamper back to locate the rug. "I don't want to stop, but give me a second, okay?" I squeezed her arms and dropped my knees, pulling out the rug then the blankets. She helped me set up a nest, then slid her hands up my thighs, working on my belt buckle. I watched her in silence, then rested my hands over hers, halting her motions. "Cass."

She looked up at me. "Yeah?"

"You don't have to do that."

"But I want to." Her head tipped to one side. "You gave me everything last time. I want to do the same for you now. Plus after last night, you kind of deserve it."

My throat tightened. "I didn't win anything, Cass." Yet again I proved just how easy it was to fall off a bull in my own personal style. I was getting pretty good at it actually.

"I didn't care if you won or not, Will. I cared if you came back to me. That was all." Her thumb brushed across my plain silver buckle, then pulled it open. I let out a fragmented breath, struggling with not fisting her hair and pulling her up my body or shoving her down onto the mat and tearing both our clothes off then and there.

Instead, I fisted my hands at my sides and waited. "You know how to torture a man."

"I had a good teacher." Her gaze flicked up to meet mine. "Someone taught me recently how to wait. Again and again and again..."

Her palm grazed my cock through my jeans, and just as quickly the contact disappeared, leaving me without the pressure I craved. I let out a groan, needing to be on my knees between her legs.

"I'll get to the begging stage real soon," I murmured, reaching out to stroke her hair, sweeping blonde waves back from her face. "You know I'm gonna want you bad after you tease me like this."

Her eyes flashed her defiance. "Slow was fun, Will. But sometimes fast and rough is just as good."

This. Girl.

Blood surged south. The moment her hands closed around my length I thought I'd end up disgracing myself. Then her lips closed around my cock and I was fucked. Royally. I fisted her hair, wrapping the pale blonde strands around my knuckles as she sucked on me, playing with balls and teasing the ever loving fuck out of me.

I gritted my teeth, tipping my head back to study the stars between the tree tops. I knew if I watched her, I wouldn't be able to stop myself from spilling my seed straight down her throat. The vision of my length disappearing between her lips was too damn good, even in the reflected light from the full moon that made it between the trees. The river helped and the clearing gave me the perfect visual on a clear night.

My cock flexed as she sucked hard, bobbing her head. I let out a groan and gripped her hair, pulling her up to me.

"Tease me another time, honey," I murmured. "Right now, I need to see you. Strip for me." It wasn't a question and I didn't pose it as one.

Cassie watched me, her breaths shallow and short as she dropped her jacket in a heap at one corner of the rug. Her shorts followed and I drank in the sight of my girl in her bra and jeans.

"Pants, too," I murmured, unbuttoning my sleeves and my shirt, letting it hang open for now as I ditched my jacket. I didn't care how cold it was, but she might in a minute.

Kneeling as she peeled off her jeans. I grabbed a blanket without looking, needing to memorize the sight of her naked for all the months we'd be apart while she was at college.

"Come here," I murmured, flicking my fingers forward.

Cassie walked straight over to me, not the least self-conscious, and my cock stiffened painfully in my jeans. She planted one foot either side of my hips and lowered herself so she knelt over me, and rocked her weeping pussy over my denim covered cock.

"Fuck," I whispered cupping her hips with my lightest touch, watching her breasts bounce with every movement. "Christ, you're beautiful."

Cass gave me the smallest smile and tugged at my shirt. "You're overdressed."

I tossed my shirt and pressed her back onto the rug, kicking my jeans free. "Can I fuck you raw, honey? I won't last as long, but I'm aching to fill you up."

She shivered at my words. "I want to ride you," she whispered, her cheeks darkening.

I hovered above her. "Show me."

Light hands pressed to my hips, she pushed me down until my back hit the mat. Then she rolled her curvy body over mine and straddled me, rubbing her saturated little pussy over my cock.

"Fuck, that's beautiful." I cupped her breasts in my palms, rolling the nipples. "Condom's in my jeans. Otherwise, I'm all yours, honey."

Cass let out a shuddering breath as I played with her and reached for me. She gave my cock an experimental pump, then lifted her hips, rubbing the head through her wetness. A soft cry ripped from her as she impaled herself on my length, then started to slide down me.

My hands flew to her hips, aching to control her descent. "I don' t want to hurt you," I groaned, trying to hold back the need to coat her insides on the spot.

"It's not sore. Just so fucking good," she gasped, her pussy clenching down tight on me."

"Yeah" I squeezed her hips and pushed her down another inch and swore she screamed. "Now, fuck me with that tight little pussy, Cass. All the way up and all the way back down. I want to feel your soft ass cheeks resting on my balls, or I'll flip you over and use my tongue from your back entrance all the way to your pussy.

I sore the hole in question clamped down on me tightly. She even gushed a little. A moan ripped from her lips and I smirked.

"You like talking dirty, huh? I'll remember that." Maybe she was filthier than I thought. I could live with that.

Her body rocked slowly over my cock. I gritted my teeth at how tight she was, clamping around me.

"Will..." A breath shuddered from her as she rode me slowly. "I think I'm–" Seconds later I swore she detonated over me from the inside out. Heat suffused my cock, liquid gushing over her thighs and mine as she squirted on me.

"Christ." I gripped her throat and pulled her tight to me for the sort of kiss I swore to myself years ago I'd only ever reserve for one woman.

Cassie gasped in my hold as I clamped my other hand to her hip and bucked up into her, again and again, fucking her until her cries melded with mine. We worked together, riding fast and hard and rough until I swore my balls were fit to burst, but there was no way that I would come before she did.

Casie shivered around me again. I leaned up, capturing her nipple in my mouth and sucked, flicking the top with my tongue.

She screamed, slamming down onto me as she tipped her head back. Heat gripped me a second time, her flutters close as she milked me. I let out a long groan, my balls beyond the tingling stage as I came. Pleasure rippled through my body in a high beyond epic. So far beyond.

"Come here." I tucked the borrowed blanket around us, needing her close. "Not gonna let you go, pretty girl. Not gonna let you go all night. I promise, alright, Cass?" I stared into bright blue eyes and prayed she'd let me take her back to school. Prayed she'd let me come and pick her up at the end of term, too. Or semester. Or whatever she studied. I'd be there at the end, as long as she still wanted me afterward.

"I love you," I murmured, grazing my lips along her neck.

"You're crazy, " she whispered still sighing and catching her breath.

"Probably." I sank into the rug, the blanket next and wrapped her tight in my arms, pulling the blankets over us.

Everything else, including food could wait. She came first in this, and all I needed right now was her. I wrapped her in my arms until my eyes shut and I fell asleep, knowing I'd finally sleep well for a night and wake without an alarm going off in my ear.

And when I did wake, the forest was full of smoke, the wildfire's heat not so far away.

CHAPTER FOURTEEN

WILL

The green wood forest that looked romantic yesterday darkened around us, shadows I thought I recognized filtering through the smoke. Now would be a good time for winter to come on early. I needed it to start fucking snowing *today*. Or deluge the mountain in one hell of a cloudburst. But I couldn't see the mountain or the granite rock face through the billowing haze, and so no one could hear my choked up prayer.

The moment I saw the smoke I pulled my clothes on, tugging Cassie's over her head without explanations. I grabbed our phones, but that was it, those and our boots were all we took. I gripped Cassie's hand too tight, tugging her along behind me, my strides lengthening until I broke into a run.

"Will –" Her voice already came out scratchy. I cursed and inhaled two deep breaths, coughing on the thick smoke obscuring the air around us and choking out every inch of remaining oxygen.

It didn't matter that we couldn't feel the heat of the fire that was probably half a mountain away at this point. It didn't matter that the flames wouldn't reach because the damn smoke would kill us at this rate. We were miles into the forest —we walked a long way last night—and what seemed like a romantic afternoon together yesterday was fast turning into a hell I could never have predicted.

Everything Trav tried to warn me about since I noticed that first thin column of smoke the day we arrived at Red Hart. This is the season...

"Will!" A new voice joined Cassie's, followed by a plethora of coughing.

A fresh version of hell closed up my chest.

"Miss Eve." A gripped Cassie tighter, towing her across the forest in a different direction instead of ploughing through the trees towards the Homestead, searching for the new voice as water streamed from my eyes. "Where the hell are you?"

She could cuss me out later for my language. Right now that seems less of an inconvenience to her. We needed to get out of this. Branches crackled and crashed around us at a not so far distance. *Shit* Maybe the fire was closer than I thought. Something sliced my face. I snapped twigs off as I went, creating a bear track of carnage with a little mini tornado flurrying behind me.

Cassie's barefoot stumbles rent at me but we couldn't stop. She hadn't been able to locate her boots in the smoky hazy before we left and time mattered. We already lost minutes by tracking sideways through the trees rather than towards our destination.

"Eve," I hollered again.

"Will." The call came fainter but closer this time.

"Fuck." I stumbled into a small hollow and to my knees beside her where she crouched, her arms wrapped around her auburn head to block out the smoke as she coughed up what sounded like part of a lamb. "Christ, girl."

"Here." Cassie offered me her cardigan to wrap around her face. I took it gratefully, but that left Cassie with little protection as she kept her hands around her face, throwing her hair over her eyes but it was nowhere near enough to ward off the tendrils of smoke that wound their way into every crevice as she crouched next to Eve.

"Come on, Eve. We have to keep moving," I encouraged her in a thin voice punctuated by her own slight coughs.

When Cassie glanced up at me, I offered her a slim smile, proud of my girl for her bravery. Proud that she wasn't focusing on her body on this day of panic and horrors. How many miles we needed to cover to get the hell out of this mess was both critical and a total mind fuck. Because suddenly my one burden that I might've pulled out of the forest had become two.

Cassie reached for us as I gathered Eve in my arms, and stopped when she coughed again. She fixed watery eyes on me. "Your shirt. Will, give me your shirt," she demanded, bringing me out of my daze.

I spluttered out half a laugh, half a cough in the fast thickening smoke. Fuck, if I didn't get the girls out of here soon, we're weren't going to make it back to the house. Just how far we had to go settled over me in a chill that busted through the permeating heat of the smoke blanket, waking me up. I focused on Casie's sass, gathering Eve in my arms. "I don't think this is the time to request a show." I tried to wave away the smoke between us.

She shook her head. "I'm not trying to get you to display anything, cowboy," she sassed me back. "Give me your damn shirt."

Frowning, I undid a few buttons and shucked it off over my head. She shook her head as I did the rest of the button then tossed it to her.

"Catch," I called, suddenly half naked with a girl in my arms and no shirt on. Embers began to flitter around us, tiny ones that bit into my skin. "Fuck. Shit."

"That language," Eve managed between coughing fits, her hands cupped around her mouth.

"Okay, we're moving." Making the call not to wait any longer, I hauled Eve to my chest, blown away by how light and frail she seemed when I lifted her.

At least I'll be able to run at full speed. She had to weigh in at less than forty kilos. I was pumped with adrenaline, and hopefully Cass would keep up by my side, we were gonna make it out. I was going to believe that, and we could do this.

"Here." Something wet and cold slapped me in the face, breaking into my impromptu pep talk.

"Ugh." I reached back in time to catch my wet shirt from sliding to the hazy forest floor. Cassie wrapped her wet cardigan over her face. "Sorry, I didn't have one for you," she apologized. "That's for Eve. She's pregnant, Will." Her words came out muffled but there were words all the same.

"She's– fuck." Something colder than a wet shirt hit me a gut level.

"Language."

I smiled down at the muddy wet blob against my chest. Eve stopped coughing and breathed against my chest. "It's enough. Right now we gotta run, girl. You gonna do that for me?" I knew Cassie hated running, exercise of any sort, but right now we didn't have a choice.

"I'll match your steps."

"Good girl." I gave her the sort of smile that promised her a reward at the other end. When we got there. I looked down at the muddy blob and started to move. "Honey, I need you to sing to that baby in your belly." The words seemed foreign to me. No wonder she'd been trying to get Archer back here. *Fuck.* I kept my opinions to myself. "I need you to tell me everything that you're gonna do with him and Archer when he gets here. Because he is coming back. You remember? You told me so. Last Christmas."

Cassie's breath hitched behind beside me. That was a story we could talk about later. On the drive back to college, maybe. She deserved the truth of what happened here that year. "You like to sing, right? So sing to your baby, Miss Eve. Sing all the way back to the house. I know your voice is gonna hurt but it only has to be soft."

I needed her to talk. I needed the vibrations or something to tell me that she was still alive under there and not suffocating while I ran. I wouldn't have the breath to keep talking to her shortly. I walked fast as my pace picked up and I started to jog.

Cass matched me, footfall for footfall, as the smoke thickened and the embers showered us in a heavier rain, obscuring my vision. My lungs and my throat burned, and I knew I'd never get rid of that scent or that smell or the taste of ash on my tongue. Everything I ate from now on would taste burnt forever. Ash would coat everything from my blood to the dust and dirt at the rodeo.

Twigs and branches scratched my face as I ran.

Pine needles caught alight from the floating embers, searing burns across my cheeks but I couldn't raise my arms to stop them. Strands of my hair drifted past, the stink assailing my senses. They were probably no longer attached to my head. Cassie pounded the ground beside me until her steps faltered, and her footsteps fell a little behind.

"Keep up, girl," I gasped out, managing to control my next coughing fit. That's all I had and I couldn't talk after that, pushing through burning lungs made up of the smoke and air that I swore combusted with every overheated breath.

The big house will be there. Travis will be there they'll be fighting. No one will stop.

I can't stop. We can't stop. And inside my arms the bundle of two, baby and mumma hummed.

All without coughing. A miracle if I could pull off any of that. But the material draped around Eve, protecting her and her baby, started to dry. The mud kept the material wet somewhat around her head, heavy adding to my burden but it didn't matter. I held her anyway and I kept trying. Something crashed behind me but I kept my foot steady, pushing through.

A burning pain seared through my legs that went

numb when oxygen no longer mattered. Because I could see it.

Fuck, I could see the damn house and it was not on fire.

I had maybe a field to go to get there. The one I walked across with a Cass last night before we started our nighttime picnic.

Travis stood somewhere on the roof and every piece of equipment that Red Hart owned stood in the center of the big field, near the barn. The whole thing looked wet. By the time I broke through the trees and stumbled across the paddock through the herd he must've emptied every water tank Red Hart owned around the house and the barn, protecting the herd and the house. And all the farm equipment—tractors, the irrigation system, everything. It was all safe.

"Travis." My voice finally gave out as my legs did. Someone saw me, maybe Jude or Gage, I couldn't tell from the stinging in my eyes, and started to sprint towards me. "We made it." One leg turned to jelly. I dropped a knee. I peeled the material back from Eve's face where she still sang quietly against my chest. Someone pried Eve's form out of my arms. I looked up into Travis's tear stained face.

"You brought her back." He stared at me. "We

didn't know where she was. She hadn't taken a truck but she fucking walked in, looking for something she'd left out there the day before. I didn't know –" His throat closed up the same as mine.

"Yes sir," was all I could get out.

Rough hands gripped my shoulders. My feet found dirt and miraculously stayed standing. I stared at Jude, his jaw locked.

"Looks like the fire stayed over the hill and all we got was smoke. Some of the back fields might be fucked but we got the car."

"Car?" I frowned at him.

"That way." He pointed to the north western boundary that I knew they shared a common fence line with a neighbor they didn't always get alone with. "Looks like someone set something alight on purpose. I've been chasing those bastards for fucking hours." Jude's usual animosity came out to play as he joined us. He frowned at me. "Where's Cassie?"

I blinked and held out a hand, turning. "She's right –" *Here.*

The last word died on my lips as I surveyed the space behind me and stared back at Forest.

Fuck.

"Where's my sister?" Austin charged up to us, resembling the carnage of the night before.

Gage's fist caught him dead centre in the chest and knocked him back half a dozen paces. "Not the fuck now, Maguire. Wait your turn."

I turned back to the fire even as my legs wobbled. The smoke thickened with a breeze that brought the heat with it, toward the house. "There was a crash," I said as I stumbled forward. "I don't know what happened. Maybe something came down. I gotta find her." I surveyed the forest, trying to pick out where the hell I came out of the tree line but the smoke obscured everything. "I think I came out there."

"You're not going back in there, Will."

Behind us, Eve puked on the ground.

"Christ, she's bleeding," Travis panted.

Jude glanced between us. "I'll help you," he gripped my hand, lifting me off the ground with a simple grip when I could barely help myself stand.

I shook my head. "You're needed here," I snapped. "I've got Cass."

The heaviest weight I'd ever felt pressed on the back of my neck like a morality check before it slammed into my spine. "We've got Cass." I'll cast a glance sideways at Austin and nod.

"We do."

The muscle of my legs had one more ride in

them. I took off towards the fire that came running down the hill towards me.

Slower, or faster – I had no idea. Pinpointing on the place I wanted to go because that's all I had to do. "She's gotta be there. She's got to be there," I chanted.

Two sets of footsteps pounded the ground beside me. I didn't have words left in my lungs as my eyes streamed to fresh. The tree line came up faster than before and then we were back in the thick of it. Running into the smoke was nothing like running from it. I didn't even know where she was. The crash I was looking for didn't just pop up. I searched for something that had a fallen pink cardigan. The one with strawberries on it – I bent down at the ground level scattering about my hands trying to find her. A hand grabbed my neck, yanking me back up right away.

"Fuck off. Get down here and help me." Finally, Austin got the message, getting to his knees beneath the layer of smoke and helping. My hands burnt my fingertips screaming at me. My jeans tore and singed at the knees. Something landed on my bare back. I yelped and tasted iron but I didn't stop, not until my hands came across something soft, something almost damn cuddly. "Cassie."

I resisted tugging at it. Her eyes closed in her sleep, her face soft beneath the smoke.

No, no no no no no no no no no no no no no no no no fuck no.

The thought filled my mind, racing around as I stroked her hair covered in ash and pine needles. Then her eyes fluttered and my heart stalled in my chest.

"Will." Her face was covered in dirt and streaks, and half her body lay beneath the vee of two branches that come down together on top of each other. I cupped my hands around her face, leaning down far enough to kiss her and nearly overbalanced, bashing our faces gently together

"Found you," I murmured

"Fucking help," Gage groused.

I looked up to find him gripping one end of a log and grasped the other. We rolled it off her together as I held onto her body, checking for damage but there was nothing visible thankfully.

I couldn't tell if she was bruised or just battered but she didn't seem to be bleeding anywhere, thank God. The next log came off just as easily though she groaned as the branch came up and I found her. "At least I'm not the only one with a busted shoulder now," I croaked.

Then Gage was there, lifting her. "I got her." Blonde hair brushed my face as they disappeared into the haze. I sat in a divot of pine mulch and ash, and waited as the fire warmed my filthy, scratched and burned back.

"Nah, you ain't dying here, fucker." Austin gripped my chest then the world levitated.

"Put me down. I can run."

"No, you can't."

Then the forest moved, taking us both with it. My body bumped along over his shoulders while my eyes streamed and drool dripped from my mouth that my arms were too tired to wipe away. Embers singed my back as we both hissed with the pain, and he cursed more than I did. Finally, the air cleared enough for us both to hack oxygen into our lungs that attempted to work again. He crawled the last few paces while I fell face first into the mud, and blessedly sank my face into it at Cassie's feet. She stoked my burn back with wet cloths with her good hand while I tried not to scream and held her toe with my pinkie, fucking glad we were alive.

And who knew? Austin turned out to be a hero. Stranger things had happened.

Maybe I could stay on a bull after all.

EPILOGUE

WILL

I didn't get another chance to stay on a bull at Red Hart but there were plenty of chances to ride again with the next rodeo circuit coming up. Before I did any of that, first I had to keep a promise to a pretty girl I'd fallen in love with beneath a mountain that watched us all, even if that wasn't where we'd be staying.

"I'm gonna take you home," I told Cassie one day well after the first snows of winter set in coating Red Hart in the same blanket of white I'd seen it in that first Christmas when I fell in love with that piece of land. It reverberated with something deep within me that this was also where I'd fallen in love with the girl of my dreams. And now, I had something else on my mind too. "I know it's real late in the season for you to head back, but I figured they might take you with your good grades and all."

I wrapped my arms around her, nuzzling her neck as she sipped tea on the veranda, watching the early season snowflakes fall. Cassie reached out to catch a tiny flake on her fingertip. Its perfectly formed shape was unique, just like her. I savored the moment we stole alone, memorizing the shape of her pressed to me. Everyone else was either inside the big house, or out working. It was cold but not too cold, not yet, though I figured it was about to be.

"You're breaking up with me on a cross state road trip?"

I sensed her smile to soften her words as I studied her fingertip, the snowflake I swore she caught a moment before already gone.

"Melted already?' I asked with sympathy. "I

promise there will be plenty more soon." *I'm not breaking up with you.*

"Only if we stay." *Are you making me leave?*

"Only if we stay." *I'll never force you to do anything, beautiful girl.*

"You can't hide here forever."

But I want to, just to stay with you.

"Maybe one day we could find somewhere to call home. Like this."

"Says the boy who doesn't know how to put roots down."

Ouch. That one almost stung. "You're in a mood. What's going on?" I asked her gently, stroking my fingers along her jaw as I tipped her head back and stole her ability to talk as I kissed her gently.

A soft, breathy sigh left her lips as she stared up at me. "I don't know what I was saying."

I laughed, deep and low, my mouth an inch from hers. "I want to take you across the state to college, and come pick you up in semester break to join the rodeo crew or come here between times. Until I'm done. Then maybe we can find somewhere together. It'll never be fancy," I stared at her, willing her to understand what I couldn't say. "I'll never have a big salary. Your parents will be disappointed."

She stared right back at me hard. "That's always

bugged me, you know. That I care what they think. That it's about them. Not me. What if, for the first time, I just went to college, did what I wanted, and graduated? No more pressure from anyone. And what if I fell in love with a cowboy of my choosing. What about that, Will Kirk?"

She sauntered around me in a circle, placing her tea on the veranda railing.

"I'd say do what it is you want to do," I said carefully. *Just please let that be with me.*

I held my breath as she completed her circuit. "If you want to stay with me?" She licked her lips. "I kept wondering when you'd dump me at college and leave and...never come back."

I gathered her into my arms. "I never agreed to that, Cassie. That was never a part of the deal," I warned her. "You're stuck with me for a whole lot longer than a few fast weeks during the off season. Okay?"

"Okay," she whispered, leaning into me.

I caught her hand and held it into the snowfall, letting her catch as many snowflakes as she wanted and showed her how to save a few in her chilled tea mug once it emptied out.

My girl. The perfect girl.

She was still finding her feet, and I didn't have a

place to call home. A few people let us stay around though and until we figured ourselves out, maybe that would be enough.

Or maybe being together was plenty.

Right now, we had the rodeo crew who looked after us, and Red Hart sure as hell wasn't going anywhere any time soon.

I grinned and lowered my mouth to hers as the snowflakes melted in her tea cup.

Yep, I had a plan. Several, actually, of what I wanted to do with this girl. And we had a whole state of travel to test it all out.

As long as she wanted to stay with a rodeo rider who didn't know how to keep his feet out of the dust while he found place of his own.

Thank you for reading Will and Cassie's story. Please leave a REVIEW.

Want to find out how Cassie met Will Kirk at that rodeo that they left right before chapter one (where he had an epic run in with Austin)?
Read KICKING UP DIRT here for FREE

The final book in Red Hart Ranch closes with Eve and Archer's last story. Read on for a glimpse of the first chapter of MISTLETOE ON THE RANGE.

Mistletoe on the Range

CHAPTER ONE

ARCHER

My last trip across the country haunted me as icy wind blasted my face. The mountainous regions of Montana came up fast after so long in the seat. My ass was numb, but every other part of me ached for the woman I hadn't seen in too long.

Damnit, I left this too late. Chasing down the man who haunted us both, tying up loose ends. The two day drive had become four between never ending road works and my own exhaustion.

Until I left Texas I hadn't realized how thin I'd left myself on energy, and spent the hours stuck in traffic battling exhaustion. Pulling in for the night after just a few hundred miles into my trip had been more than frustrating, but it was pointless to continue pushing myself when I'd only end up as another blockage on the side of the highway, a statistic lost in the multitudes of holiday traffic. Hell, half of the US seemed to be traveling north for Christmas.

Disappointing Eve had been the hardest part.

My phone vibrated in its holder beside the steering wheel. I flicked my gaze from the road to the screen, which lit up with my little hellion's name.

My hellion, because she had been raising hell for the past three days while I tried to make it across the country to her.

I'd left to chase my own demons across the country, and gotten stuck in my job down south, ensuring the man who had damaged her would never be free, when her grief had hit her hardest.

When she needed me most.

She'd had to rely on others for comfort, while I worried that the woman at the top end of the country had grown tired of waiting for me, or had decided she needed a man closer to her home.

Shoving the doubts aside, I read her message. Another flash beneath it, and I let out a laugh.

> Eve:Tell me you're at least in the right state.
>
> Eve:Don't make me come down to Texas and haul your Ranger butt back here.

Shaking my head, I shot off a quick reply, knowing she likely would jump in that white F250 and drag me back home to her. Damn cavewoman. Those doubts should have stayed in Texas.

I typed with my eyes half on the road, trailing behind an infinite line of traffic that thinned the further north I drove. Thumb fumbling words, I sent back my location, and a second later, my phone buzzed.

"Eve?" I picked it up, the steering wheel jerking

in my hands as I destroyed already totaled roadkill. "Dammit." That was going to stink later on.

"Rhys Archer. Is that how you usually answer the phone?" Eve laughed at me, though there was a tiny tremor at the end of her words.

Grinning to myself, I managed to avoid the next road bump that used to be an animal. "Nah, just trying not to run over the locals."

"You're messaging and driving?" Eve squawked through the line. Static filled the cab of my truck. "What sort of cop are you?"

I pressed my lips together, debating how to best answer that one, but regardless of what I wanted to say, there was only one real answer. "The Texas Ranger sort, honey."

Eve was silent for a long moment. I glanced away from the road, but the line was still connected.

"I'm glad you're coming back, Archer. It's...been a little while."

"Eve, I've been trying to get back since the day I left Red Hart. You. But the job was there, and I couldn't just walk away."

Lies. All lies. Because I had, anyway. I walked away from her, chased a murderer across the country, then took over a year to fight my way back.

"Work." Eve said the single word like it was a prayer and a curse.

"Always. Do you ever stop?" I asked lightly. "How's everything going in the lead up to Christmas?"

"Winding down, as always. I still miss Dad." If there hadn't been tears in her voice, there were now, and I cursed myself for being so blasé.

"I know, honey. I'll be there soon. Maybe tomorrow morning. I keep thinking it's just hours on the road, but there's so much damn traffic. I should have come earlier."

"You should've," Eve agreed in a thick voice, and I knew she was crying. "I've missed you."

"I've missed you too, Sweetheart. It's been so long you'll have to show me around again." The joke meant to soothe her fell flat. "Eve?"

"Some things are different around the ranch, Archer. It's...not quite the same as before. It's changed. I've changed."

My stomach plummeted. "Are you okay, Eve? I'll push through, maybe get there around two, a bit after midnight."

Dammit all. I should've walked away and gotten my ass to my girl earlier.

If she still *was* my girl.

"Don't be silly." The smile in Eve's voice was contagious. "Get here when you can. Don't be an accident we hear about instead."

"Alright, honey. Do you need me to get anything in town on the way through?"

"If you're coming through White Cap, can you stop at Beanies? The coffee shop. I'm not sure if you remember it," she said hesitantly.

It was where I had met her. Nothing in this world could make me forget that. "I remember."

"Oh, good. I'll put an order in with Suzy, if you'll pick it up for me?"

"Not a problem. I'll stop and get it to you tomorrow, Eve."

I'll get to you tomorrow.

"Okay." She paused. "Archer, I'm— just, be safe. Please?"

My heart lodged in my throat, I stared through the windscreen at the taillights of the car in front of me. "Will do. Take care, until I'm there with you."

"Bye, Archer."

I blinked at the road, zoned out long after she hung up. There was so much that she hadn't said. My mind flew through different options.

Losing her Dad had been hard, and that had

been at Christmas, too. Then she'd lost her mom, soon after. That was plenty of change. But surely she would have told me if she had been struggling with the ranch...well, no. With Eve Beaumont, the chances of that were less than zero. I held back a laugh; Eve hadn't accepted help, even when she'd needed it.

And now, I hadn't been there when she did.

Cursing myself as an idiot, my mind ran through the remaining options, and halted.

Hell, had she been pregnant, and not told me? Surely her brother would have called me for that.

Fixing my focus on the road in front of me, I pressed my foot down, overtaking the car in front as soon as I had space.

And the next.

The lines between the lanes blurred as the moon rose overhead, a ghost behind a blanket of snow laden clouds. It had been a dry run so far, but the weather had only held out in my favor until I hit the mountains.

I switched the heat up, and could swear ice was forming at the corners of my windshield, though that could have been my eyes. Shaking my head, I stared at the lights that announced a small town—little more than a truck stop with a hotel at the back of it. A row of rooms for rent lined the back.

As much as it would probably be a rotten night's rest in a dingy room, it was still better than sleeping in my truck in potential snow conditions.

A few vehicles were lined up for the pump. I pulled in, swiping a hand across my eyes. Pushing through to Red Hart tonight had never been a solid plan, especially if Eve needed me to pick up supplies on the way through.

White Cap was two and a bit hours from Red Hart Ranch; if I got some sleep now and didn't dally in town I could be there just after lunch.

The pump freed up. I filled my thirsty truck—or maybe I'd been too heavy on the gas—and headed into the store to pay and organize a room for the night.

My stomach rumbled.

Even a Ranger had needs he couldn't ignore. And Eve...seeing her again was a whole new level of desire. The ghost of her silken curls itched my palms. I pressed them to my hips at the memory, a stupid grin spreading over my face.

I stopped behind a man dressed in black, lost in

my fantasy of the woman I loved spread naked on my bed, until he turned around. My grin soured and slid from my face.

Eve's creepy as fuck neighbor stared at me with dislike.

The feeling's mutual, Black Hill boy.

We hadn't gotten along well the last time I'd been at Red Hart, though it was for a very different reason than I travelled for now.

The tall cowboy had a habit of wearing black and loitering around his father's ranch. Red Hart and Black Hill shared miles of fence line that often seemed to have issues with stock staying on their own side, and the rancher's son was habitually involved. Plus, I hadn't liked the way he affected Eve.

"Pierce." I nodded, fixing my gaze at a point between his eyes.

"Archer." A slow smile stretched his lips.

If he'd been in Texas, I would have arrested him for breathing.

"Good to be back in Montana."

"Is it? Are you staying long?" Pierce half turned away, throwing his face into sharp relief beneath flickering fluorescent lights.

"Long enough to become a fixture." I slipped my hand into my pocket before I punched him for no reason. Pierce had always rung alarm bells for me, and those little tinklers had saved my life god knew how many times.

"Might find some things have changed up on the mountain." Pierce paid the cashier, tipping his hat to be. "Have a safe drive back."

My stomach clenched; hadn't Eve said the same thing earlier? More than anything, I wanted to get up to Red Hart, to hold her and make sure she was alright, but I needed to sleep. And driving in the middle of the night while I was pissed and distracted by Pierce wouldn't do myself any favors.

"Sir?" The cashier called, his gaze darting between me and the doors that swung shut behind the tall cowboy.

I paid the man, sorting accommodation and a meal to take back to my room. Company didn't suit me anymore. Swallowing a bitter aftertaste that lingered in my mouth, I headed back to my truck with instructions of where to park for the night.

As I neared my truck, my teeth began to grind.

A long stripe that shouldn't have been there was carved into the perfect red paintwork, reaching as deep as bare metal, the edges irregular, like the tip of a key.

I clenched my teeth harder, an instant headache blooming at my temples.

Fucking Black Hill boy.

It looked like I wasn't going to get a lot of sleep tonight, after all.

Archer's story will conclude in MISTLETOE ON THE RANGE.

RECIPES

RANCH HAND'S COTTAGE PIE

PIE

- 1kg chuck steak
- 1 kg minced beef
- 2 brown onions roughly chopped
- 2 tins roma tomatoes
- 4 garlic cloves crushed and chopped
- 2 stems rosemary
- 4 stems basil, leaves plucked

4 large mushrooms, roughly chopped

2 carrots, skinned and chopped

Peas to serve on top.

Cook in 2-4L of water until fat on beef is rendered and pulls away when stirred. Liquid should appear glossy and thin, with a red/orange sheen from the tomatoes. Boil until liquid reduces for 2-3 hours.

POTATO TOPPING

8-10 potatoes skinned and chopped.

Sour cream to taste

Boil unrtil soft. Drain and mash. Add sour cream to taste and whip to consistency by hand. Serve on top of meat mixture and top with peas.

Severs 8

POTATO AND LEEK SOUP

8 large potatoes, skinned

1 leek finely chopped

Four bacon rashes chopped

Two tablespoons garlic

One brown onion finely diced

Boil in 2L of water for 1-2 hours. Top up water as needed. Add 1-200ml heavy cream to taste and blend in saucepan. Serve immediately with warmed buttered rolls or bread.

Serves 6-8

ABOUT THE AUTHOR

USA Today Bestselling author Sofia Aves writes fast-paced police romances, sizzling military units, steamy cowboys with a Montana backdrop and the occasional cheeky god. Sofia writes kidlit for charity and has over one hundred and fifty publications across five not-so-super-secret pen names. As acquisitions editor for Evernight and Evernight Teen publishing she loves discovering new talent in romance and YA spaces, and is a mum of three crazies in a returned veteran household. Sofia has two overly large fur babies who think they're teacup puppies, a duck who prefers to eat from a dog bowl and two axolotls named after a dragon and a firebird.

Sofia lives near Brisbane, Australia where she has her own alpaca park, Lorendel.

www.sofiaaves.com

Sign up to Sofia's newsletter and get a free Blue Blooded Brothers book.

Haven't read the Z Boy's prequel? Get it for free here:
A TABLE FOR TEN

Follow Sofia on
BookBub
Twitter
Instagram

Read Sofia's Series

Blue Blooded Brothers
  Collision
  Politics & Paperwork
 Blindsided
 Sentinel
 Mugshots & Candy Canes
 Impact
 Reckoning

Red Hart Ranch
 Snow on the Range
 Siren on the Range
 Sundown on the Range
 Spirit on the Range

Ash on the Range (2025)
Mistletoe on the Range (2025)
Forgotten Mountain Man

Texan Devils

Ranger's Wish
Ranger Bedevilled
Ranger's Passion
Ranger's Fury
Ranger's Wrath
Ranger's Storm
Snapdragons & Seductions
Summer with a Ranger
Merry with a Ranger

Playing to Win

Off Boarding
Vicious Slash
Zero Pointer
Off Stage Fling

Rippton Allstars

Crushing It

Glacial Force

Rippton Creatives

Study Games

Make Me, Break Me

Twisted Obsession

Spring Break with a Mafia Prince

A Royally Fake French Menage

Jericho Chimeras

Puck Me Always

Puck My Heart

Puck me Sideways

Z Boys

King

Joker

Hearts

Ace

Mayhem & Mistletoe

Ruski

. . .

Fast Track to Love
Speed Trap

Klauss Brothers
Zander
Keegan

Gallo Empire *with Jade Marshall*
Splintered Vows
Fractured Vows
Fierce Vows
Savage Covenant

Rom Coms
She's A Hot Christmas Mess
Boats, Moats and Root Beer Floats

Writing Romantasy as
SOFIA SHELLEY
Dead Poets Sorority

. . .

Writing Reverse Harem Dark Romance as
DOVE PRIEST
Recurve Ridge

Kidlit writing as
JO SEYSENER
The OCD Elf
The OCD Elf's Great Reindeer Calamity
Greg and the Egg

writing YA as
JOSS PHOENIX
Alchem Academy (2025)

Writing spicy paranormal romance as
RAVEN HUSH

Club Fray
Darkest Desires
Purge
Kidnapped By Claws
Ruin

. . .

Shadow Lords
Sinner's End
Heaven's Gate (2026)

Monster Brides
Phoenix's Eternal Flame
Kraken's Vow
Krampus' Christmas Bride

Silent Sentinels Duet
Reflections of Silence
Echoes in the Void

Monsters In New York
Feral Moon Rising (2025)